Carpe Diem

A STORY OF LOVE AND ADVENTURE

RAE MATTHEWS

Carpe Diem
Copyright © 2016 Rae Matthews

Edited by: Kerry Genova, Writersresourceinc.com
Cover Design: Rae Matthews
Formatting: Rae Matthews
Pipers Tattoo Designed by: Wendy Oleston
Author Photo by: BC Fotos, Minneapolis, MN

***

ISBN-13:
978-1523298600

ISBN-10:
152329860X

Dedication

For all those who have forgotten there is more to life then
working to pay the bills, doing the dishes, folding the
laundry, or bitching out the asshole that stole your parking
spot when they could clearly see you were waiting for it.

SEIZE THE DAY

CONTENTS

Acknowledgments

Seize the day is not just a phrase but also a way of thinking that should be embraced each and every day. It doesn't matter if you take just an extra moment to kiss a loved one good-bye, if you take a trip to the zoo with your kids for the first time, or even if you just stop and literally smell the roses. Each day has a moment in it that should be seized and cherished, if even just for a moment. The important thing is that you stopped and lived in that moment.

I want to say thank you to those in my life that have helped me live in the moment. I have so many wonderful memories because of you, and since I can't name you all I will say, you know who you are, and if you don't, well, then you probably need to call me to make plans.

I wish I could share those memories with all the readers but if I did that now, I would just be writing another book so I have selected a few and have added them as part of Piper's story. Not all of her adventures are from my memories—some are my memories waiting to happen.

Chapter One
The Sky is Falling

Finding myself a widow at the age of thirty-eight was not something I ever thought could happen to me. Not that anyone ever thinks something like this will happen to them, but I was so naive about tragedy that you could have told me the sky was falling and I would have responded with, "Not over my house it isn't." It has been two years since I got the knock at the front door that burst my perfect little bubble. It all still feels like it was just yesterday.

I was finishing the morning dishes. Jack and I always had breakfast together each morning. I would get up, toss on my jeans and a tee shirt, and then head to the kitchen while Jack would get into the shower. We started this little tradition three years ago when our daughter Bryna went off to college in an effort to not fall into some kind of empty nesters funk. After the first year of bacon and eggs each morning, I decided it was time to come up with some new ideas to spice up the morning. Being that I was no culinary genius, I turned to the Internet for help. That particular morning we had orange chocolate chip waffles with orange caramel sauce and bananas with a side of bacon. It was my latest find on Pinterest. As I placed my latest creation on the table in from of us, we burst into laughter at its appearance and then stalled, waiting for the other to take the first bite. Realizing what we were doing, we decided to take the first bite together.

"One, two, three, go" I say, holding my overflowing fork.

Still sitting frozen in the same position, neither of us moved the fork closer to our open mouths and now we are attempting to hold back the laughter that is trying to break through our straight faces.

"You were supposed to go on three," Jack blurts.

"So were you!" I say with my own laughter escaping, making it hard to speak.

After two more attempts at the countdown, we both at last cave in and take our first bite together. To our surprise, it was actually damn delicious and quickly decide it needs to go into the "must make again" pile. Conversation about our plans for the day fills the kitchen as we finish our breakfast. Jack was going to the office for the morning and then he had a few off-site meetings this afternoon. I planned to start a yoga class later this afternoon, we agree that tonight will be a fend for yourself style dinner since he did not know when he would be home and I may or may not injure myself attempting some yoga pose with a fancy name like the river runs clear.

After breakfast, Jack kisses me good-bye and heads off to work while I go for my morning run. Okay, maybe run is too strong a word. It was more like a fast walk slash jog, that is until I pass by my friend Abby Reed's house. I love Abby to death, she is one of my best friends, but she is a marathon runner and gives me shit every time I *walk* past her house. So I learned that the best way to avoid that is to start running about two houses up from hers and stop about three houses after, silly I know, but it saves me from getting a giant dose of Abby style *motivation* via text messages for the next hour. Honestly, I have no idea how her husband Dave deals with it because he is most definitely not a man that cares about being in shape.

Once I determine that I have worked off enough calories for now, I make my way back home. I immediately jump in the shower and start making a mental list of all the things I had to do today. After getting out of the shower, getting dressed, and transferring my mental list into a real list, I start cleaning up my monster mess in the kitchen.

I have yet to master the art of the cleaning as you go cooking style. I was drying the last few dishes when I hear the soft, but firm knock at the door. I was not expecting anyone, and it was too early for the mail. I thought it could be my sister, Casey, who is three years younger than I am and would stop by occasionally if she had a showing in my neighborhood. Casey was one of the best real estate agents in the area, she even helped Jack and I find our house when she was just starting out, and she got us a damn good price considering the neighborhood. Unfortunately, that made her extremely busy, and between spending time with her husband Chuck and my awesome nephew Leo, it was hard for her to find time to hang out, so if she was in the area and had some time, she would swing by and say hello to her big sis.

I quickly finish drying Jack's favorite red coffee cup and head to see who it is. When I pull open the front door, I am surprised to see two uniformed police officers and Jack's friend Flynn Avery staring back at me. The officer standing closest to the door was shorter and from the amount of gray hair peeking out from under his hat, you could tell had been on the job for more years than not. The other officer standing a few steps behind him was a bit younger; he was tall and seemed to be in very good shape. He had a hint of gray mixed in with his dark brown hair that made him look very distinguished. Flynn, Jack's business partner and best friend, was standing close behind them and was avoiding eye contact with me while both officers looked at me with such serious faces. I wanted to throw up my hands and scream, "I didn't do it, I didn't do it," to lighten the mood a bit.

"Are you Mrs. Piper Reynolds?" the older officer asked.

"Yes I am, can I help you?" I ask in utter confusion, looking to Flynn for a hint as to what is going on.

"I'm Officer Johnson and this is Officer Daniels. May we come in for a moment?" he asks.

"Sure. Is there a problem?" I asked, moving aside to let them in.

"Do you mind if we take a seat in the living room?" Officer Johnson asks

"Of course, but I'm confused as to what is going on here." I look to Flynn for answers, but he is still avoiding eye contact with me.

We take a seat on the couch in the living room. My heart is pounding, and my hands are starting to sweat. I have no clue what is going on. Why are they here? Why is Flynn here? Why is he avoiding my confused gaze?

"Ma'am, I'm sorry to be the one to tell you this, but your husband has been involved in an accident," he says, leaning in close to me.

When he gets to the word accident, I realize that I have been holding my breath. I do not want to release it. As long as I am still holding my breath I can live in this one moment. The moment where I do not have to ask questions, the moment where I do not have to hear the answers they will give me. I can live in this one last moment of ignorance where he is working diligently at his desk, or taking a meeting, or sipping on his coffee as he counts the hours until he comes home to me unharmed.

"Ma'am, did you hear me?" the officer asks, his deep voice finally forcing me to release the breath I had been holding on to so tightly.

"Can you tell me if he is okay?" I ask, trying to hold back

all emotions.

I realize I asked the question for the sole purpose of letting my ears hear the words that deep in my heart I already know are coming. As the officer moves a little closer to me, my gut screams out to my mind, "You fool. They don't send two uniformed officers to knock on a door if someone only has a concussion and a few bruises."

"I'm sorry, ma'am, he expired at the scene," he tells me, reaching for my hand to comfort me.

"Are you positive?" I ask out of desperation.

"Yes, ma'am. I am very sorry for your loss." Officer Johnson answers.

"I'm sorry, that is not possible. He is at work right now—" I demand, pulling my arm back from his grasp.

"Ma'am," Officer Daniels tries to interrupt.

"Stop calling me ma'am. You have the wrong house, my husband is at work." I continue loudly as if it will change anything. I continue to ramble uncontrollably as I leap up from the couch and start pacing along the length of the room. "This is not possible. He was just here, we had breakfast, and then he went to work. You have to have the wrong house, you have the wrong Jack. It wasn't him, I'm telling you, you have the wrong person! You should be ashamed of yourselves for..."

"Piper, please, stop this." The soft voice is filled with desperation stops my rant. The voice is familiar, but it is not Officer Johnson or Officer Daniels. I look up to see that it's Flynn pleading for me to stop my uncontrollable rant. He had been so quiet, not saying a word until now and hiding in the background that I actually forgot he walked up with the police. I look deep into his eyes and I can see the tears that I have been fighting slowly forming in his eyes.

"Piper, I was with Jack when he died. I know it is hard to believe this is happening, but it was Jack, there is no mistake, it was him," Flynn tells me as I watch the tears start to roll down his cheeks.

When Flynn says Jack's name, I have no choice but to give in to the tears I have been trying so hard to fight, but with that one word, I can no longer hold them back. I start gasping for air to the point of hyperventilating and the flood of tears start falling down my face. Officer Daniels is by my side a moment later and is slowly guiding me back to the couch to take a seat.

I begin to follow his lead, but before he can sit me on the couch, another burst of emotion takes over. This time, I am overcome with anger. I scream that it is not true as my arms thrash hysterically. I begin punching the arm he had extended to me that was only a moment ago a comfort and a guide. He is a very sweet man and is doing his best to calm me, but my body has a mind of its own right now. My weak punches move from his arms to his chest as he slowly tries to wrap his arms around me. His touch is gentle, and the thought that he could at any time have me on the ground and in handcuffs before I could do anything about it calms me for a moment. He pulls me closer. My head falls to his shoulder and my river of tears take over once again. Officer Daniels lets me pour my grief out on him without saying a word, for that I am grateful. When I finally lift my head from his now soaked shoulder, I look into his eyes and see that he is in some way sharing in my pain. With that, I nod my head and I let him guide me back to the couch.

"Is there someone I can call for you?" Officer Johnson asks as he kneels down to me, taking my hand in an attempt to comfort me.

Somehow, I manage to stutter out my sister's name and point to my cell phone resting on the dining room table. Officer Johnson squeezes my hand gently, then gives Officer Daniels a nod. A few moments later, Daniels returns to the living room and informs us that my sister is on her way.

I can imagine her running out of her office, climbing into her shiny blue BMW, and running every red light to get here. Casey and I have always been close and she loved Jack almost as much as I did. Not in a creepy way, in a "you are the best brother-in-law I could ever have asked for" kind of way.

Flynn walks over and takes Officer Johnson's place at my side; my tears are as uncontrollable as his. He holds me tightly and rocks me gently as if that would somehow help. I know he is in shock too and is doing anything he can think of to help. Flynn has always been a good friend to Jack and to me.

"Piper, Jack's last thoughts were of you and of Bryna," Flynn whispers

"Oh my God, Bryna. How am I going to tell her that her father is gone?" I sob

"I can help you when you are ready, but you need to be strong for her so right now is your time, your time to let it all out, and your time to scream and yell. When you are ready, we will call her together," Flynn tells me, wiping away some of the tears.

"She is going to be devastated," I reply

"I know, and when you are both ready to hear it, Jack asked me to give you a message," Flynn tells me

Flynn is doing his best to hold back his already flowing tears as he speaks and with that, I know the message will push me over the edge. I cannot hear it right now and he knows it.

"Piper!"

The sound startles me. Flynn and I turn to the front entryway and see Abby running toward me. The tears falling from her eyes are coming to join mine.

"My God, Piper, honey. What the hell happened?" Abby asks, taking the seat next to me that Flynn has given up for her.

"I don't know, an accident of some kind, I only know he's gone," I tell her between my gasps for air.

With that, Abby turns to the officers and gives them their cue to proceed with the details. I want to stop her. The less I know, the less real it will be. I do not want it to be any more real than it is right now. There is still the one last glimmer of hope that this is all still a big mistake. I know that it is a fool's hope, but it is all I have left. Once the details come out, that hope will be lost forever.

Chapter Two

Being Strong

The quiet sounds of Casey and Abby in the kitchen talking on the phone while making dinner pulls me from my sleep. For a brief moment, I feel like the past four hours have been a nightmare that I am at last waking from. I open my eyes and see the business card of Officer Johnson sitting on the coffee table and I once again I have to fight back my tears.

Flynn agreed to go pick up Bryna. I could not bring myself to tell her over the phone. Flynn has been like a second father to her and will be able to console her much better than I can right now.

The details of the accident were enough to send me into what felt like a heart attack. My breath fell short, my heart pounded in my chest, and shooting pains would surge from my heart to my head. It was not a *gruesome* accident by the accounts of the officer, but to hear that your husband, the man you have loved and expected to grow old with is dead, because some woman was too preoccupied with putting her lipstick on to stop for a red light *is* enough to make a person go crazy.

He was only a half a block away from his office. If he had *just* been sixty seconds sooner, he might have made it through the intersection. The memories of that morning began to consume me. What if I had only taken that first bite on the first countdown, what if I had shut up about what I was going to do today, what if I had given him a longer kiss good-bye, what if I had not laid his keys and briefcase next to the door? Sixty seconds. Sixty seconds sooner or sixty seconds later would have saved his life.

"She's awake," I hear Abby say to Casey

As they both walk from the kitchen over to me, they remain silent. I cannot blame them. I mean what are you supposed to say to your friend only a few hours after she finds out her husband is dead. Casey hands me a glass filled with water. I slowly reach my arm out to take it from her but cannot seem to find the strength to lift the glass up to my mouth to drink it.

"How are you doing honey? Did you get any sleep?" Abby asks.

I am not sure how to respond. My mind tells me I should say something, but my mouth is dry and I cannot seem to find any words that could possibly fit right now. When I am finally able to take a sip of the water, it tastes good. It is as if I am drinking water for the first time. The glass empties as the cool liquid runs down my throat, and I feel as if new life is coursing through my body.

"Yes I got a little," I eventually answer.

"Good, you needed it," Casey declared.

"What do I need to do?" I ask softly.

"You don't need to do anything, honey. Not right now, not until you're ready," Casey answers me.

"Ready? When will I ever be ready?" I ask with soft desperation.

"You know what I mean. When you have had a chance to take it all in," Casey tells me as she moves to my side.

"I can't believe he is never coming home," I utter, still fighting back more tears. "Home—wait where is Bryna?" I gasp.

"Flynn called a little bit ago and he is on his way back with her. They were leaving her dorm and should be here in a few hours."

"Does she know? Did he tell her?" I ask, hoping that my baby girl would have a few more hours of ignorance.

"Yes, Flynn had to tell her. You know, Bryna, there is no way she was getting in that car until she knew what was wrong."

"I know," I say, letting my first smile since this morning form, "She is so headstrong, just like Jack is, was," I respond, fighting my tears.

"I've called everyone I can think and Jack's mom will be here tomorrow. I will pick her up at the airport about two o'clock," Abby tells me.

"Mom and Dad stopped by while you were asleep. Mom wanted to stay until you woke up, but I told her to go home with Dad," Casey says, interrupting Abby.

I love my parents, but right now I'm so glad they are not here. I do not need a house full of people watching me and asking me if I need anything five hundred times an hour. Abby and Casey know me and know that I have never dealt with all eyes on me attention very well.

"What did you guys make for dinner?" I ask as I feel my stomach yelling at me.

"We made some spaghetti. It was easy and fast," Abby tells me as she stands up and moves toward the kitchen.

"Do you want to eat at the table or in here?" Casey asks me.

I am not sure why I do not answer her as I toss the blanket off my legs and walk toward the dining room table. It is as if my legs feel like they weigh a ton, but I keep walking, determined not to let my grief take over completely.

The next few hours waiting for Bryna was filled with Casey and Abby tiptoeing around from random topic to yet an even more random topic, never landing on anything too serious. It is not hard to tell that they are unsure what to do or how to act right now. This is the first time anyone of us has had to deal with something like this.

They had already made all the necessary calls while I was sleeping and until tomorrow when the funeral home opens, there is not much to do but avoid the subject and pretend everything is fine. I wander back and forth from staring at the wall to listening to them ramble on about movies coming out, cat videos that have seen, and still debating the hotness of Johnny Depp. Time seems to move so slowly and yet so fast all at the same time.

As I fade in and out, I picture Jack sitting next to me smiling and amused. I wonder what we would be doing right now. Would we be sitting down for dinner, would we be in front of the TV watching Netflix? I try not to let myself fall into the fantasy, but it pulls at me.

"How do you greet a widow when she gets up? Good morning," Jack says

"That's the dumbest thing I've ever heard in my life," I *tell him hitting him in the arm and smiling.*

"Got you to smile didn't I?" Jack teases.

"Only because I felt bad for you, not because it was funny," I tease back

"You can do this," he tells me with a smile

"I can do what?" I ask

"You can do this," he tells me again.

"I can do what? I don't understand." I ask again.

"I love you, you can do this. You can be strong, be strong for me," he tells me and kisses me on the cheek.

Those words push me back into reality, back to Abby and Casey, back to where Jack is gone. I think of him and the words my mind told me he would say and I feel the strength building inside me. I can do this. I can be strong.

"Okay!" I shout, scaring both of them.

I stand from the table and head toward Jack's office. I grab a legal pad and a pen from his desk and walk back to the table. Tossing the items down, I walk past Casey and Abby and into the kitchen where I grab three glasses and a bottle of wine.

"We are going to make a list of all the things I have to do tomorrow and then we are going to make a list of all our favorite things we love about Jack. We are going to drink, we are going to cry, we are going to laugh, and cry some more," I demand.

Casey and Abby look at each other and then back to me, jaws to the floor.

"I don't want to hear any more conversations about how your hair grows faster in the summer than in the winter or how weird it is that dog's feet smell like Fritos," I continue.

"All right then," Abby says with a smile.

"If Jack was here he would be cracking dumb jokes and making an ass of himself to make us smile. Since he can't be here, we are going to have to do it ourselves," I continue while popping the cork from the bottle of wine.

Chapter Three
Messages

A few short hours later, I hear the front door swing open and my beautiful daughter calling out for me.

"Mom! Mom, where are you," Bryna shouts.

"In here sweetheart," I call back to her from the dining room, trying to once again fight my tears.

As Bryna comes around the corner and I can see her eyes are filled with tears I cannot save her from this time. I quietly watch as she drops her bag and runs toward me, extending her arms. Her arms surround my body when she reaches me. She is holding on so tight I think I may lose my ability to breathe, but I say nothing. I embrace her tightly in return and gently rock her as I did when she was a baby.

"I know, sweetheart, I know," I say to her softly.

"He can't be gone, he can't be," she cries out.

"I know, sweetie. I don't want him to be gone either."

"He is too young. You guys are supposed to be old and senile when you die."

"As much as you wanted that to be our future, I wanted it even more."

"It's not fair. I'm not ready for him to be gone."

"Sweetie, it was just his time. We have to cherish the memories we had with him while he was with us and not be angry about the ones we will not have."

Bryna looks at me with her wet eyes and it breaks my heart all over again. She is right; this is not how it was supposed to be. She should have had at least another thirty to forty years with her father. This is not how our time together should have come to an end. I can feel my tears fighting hard to come out, but I will not let them loose, they will not win this battle. I have to be strong for Bryna.

I am startled when I see movement in the corner of my eye. I am relieved when I quickly realize that it is Flynn. He has been patiently waiting and is now holding in his hands the bag that Bryna had dropped to the ground.

"I'm sorry I didn't mean to intrude," Flynn says.

"You are most definitely not intruding," I say and walk toward him.

I retrieve Bryna's bag from his grasp and gently lay it on the floor before embracing him. Flynn is, *was,* Jack's best friend, but actually they were more like brothers. Several years ago they went into business together. For most friendships that would have been a death sentence, but not for them. Since they were the age of ten, the two of them had formed a bond that could never be broken. When Jack told Flynn his college plans had changed and that he would be staying here with me to raise the baby, Flynn dropped out of the far from home university each of them had both been accepted to, to stay close and attend the local tech college. It was all a bit weird if you ask me, but that was the nature of their friendship. They had been friends for so long and I learned early on not to question things too much.

"Did you get much sleep?" Flynn asked

"Some, not much," I respond. "I can't thank you enough for going to pick up Bryna for me. I don't know how I can repay—" I say.

"There is no need to thank me or repay me. I am glad to help in any way I can," he interrupts.

"Thank you just the same, you are a good friend."

Flynn responds, giving me a smile and nods.

"Did you stop to eat? There is some leftover spaghetti in the fridge I can heat up for you."

"No, thank you. We went to the drive-through about an hour ago, but you might want to try and get Bryna to eat some, she didn't eat much."

"Thank you, I will."

"I really should be going," Flynn says, looking over to Bryna and then back to me

"You're welcome to stay. We are reminiscing and going through some old pictures for the service."

"I don't want to intrude, besides I could use some sleep myself."

"I understand completely. Let me walk you out."

Part of me was scared to let Flynn leave; it was nice having him here. It made me feel as if he arrived early for plans he and Jack had made and we were sitting here hanging out waiting for Jack to get home from a meeting that ran long. Once Flynn leaves, that illusion will be gone and I will have to return to reality once again.

"I will check in on you tomorrow, if that is okay," Flynn says as he steps onto the front porch.

"Thank you, that would be nice."

My eyes pop open before the sun has risen, Bryna fast asleep beside me. I don't want to wake her, she had such a hard time falling asleep, and I want her to get as much rest as she can. Today is going to be hard for both of us. I should try to get more sleep, two hours will not be enough, but my mind is awake and running through the list of things that will need to be done. Before I can talk my brain into letting me rest a little longer, my bladder starts to yell at me. With that, I carefully roll out of bed, gently placing my feet on the hardwood floor. As I tiptoe to the bathroom, I become painfully aware of how quiet and still the house has become compared to the noise and emotions it was filled with only yesterday. It vaguely reminds me of the day we moved Bryna to the dorms her freshman year. I remember Jack and I were so proud of her that day. She was able to start an adventure we did not get the chance to take.

I walk through the house, careful not to make any noise. Casey is asleep in the spare room, and Abby is asleep on the couch. I make a cup of tea and walk out onto the front porch. The neighborhood is starting to wake up, the birds are starting to sing their morning songs, the sprinklers two houses down have come on to give the grass a morning drink, and the sun is finally starting to peek over the horizon.

As I sit on my porch swing watching the sunrise, I can't help but feel a little peace for the first time since the knock at my door yesterday. The warmth of the sun heating the cool morning air, the squirrel dashing across the street to run up his favorite tree, the woman down the street that is taking her dog for a walk, it all feels so normal. The daily routines of those around me are still going on as if nothing has happened. It is the first sign that life will go on, whether I want it to or not.

"Good morning, you're up early."

The words pull me from my thoughts; it's Flynn. What is he doing here so early?

"Hey, what are you doing up at this hour?" I ask.

"I couldn't sleep," he replies.

"Have you been walking all night?" I ask, taking a sip of my tea.

"Not all night, just since about two this morning." He smiles awkwardly.

"Well, I would say close enough. Where did you go?"

"Oh here and there. Then before I knew it, I found myself

walking here."

Flynn doesn't live very far from us, I would say five miles at most. The idea of him wandering around in the middle of the night actually makes me feel better, as bitchy as that may sound. Knowing that it was not only me tossing and turning while the knock at the door replayed over and over in my head. All I could hear when I closed my eyes were the voices of the detectives telling me my husband was dead. Dead, the man I loved and planned to spend the rest of my life with was dead. The images of us growing old together were gone from my imagination. The dreams of sitting on this very porch while watching our grandkids play in the yard had been crushed.

"Hello? You in there?" Flynn asks as he waves his hand in front of my face.

"I'm sorry. I must have zoned out there for a minute," I reply, slightly embarrassed.

"I'd say, you were in a whole other dimension if I didn't know better." Flynn chuckles.

"I'm sorry I didn't get much sleep either and my mind has been wandering a lot," I explain.

"Piper, you are going to be fine. I know it doesn't feel like it right now, but you know you will get through this."

My eyes would fill with tears if I had any left. Flynn takes my hand in his as he sits next to me on the swing. They are cool to the touch, the morning air has chilled them some.

"Jack wanted you to know that he loved you with all his heart..." Flynn starts.

Now, he is going to do this now? Am I ready to hear Jack's last words in the world? My mind shudders from thought to thought, not sure if I should stop Flynn or let him finish. The words "stop, not now" are stuck in my throat unwilling to come out. I feel my hand close around his as if to silently protest.

"I know you think you are not ready. You are. You are the strongest woman I know," he continues.

My heart skips a beat and I nod to let him know it is okay to continue.

"Jack wanted you to know that he loved you with all his heart. He wanted you to know that his last thoughts were of you and that he felt lucky to have had you and Bryna in his life. He wants you to mourn him and then move on. He doesn't want you to live the rest of your life with sorrow in your heart," Flynn finishes.

My eyes are filled with tears and my heart with love for this man, this man that while he lay dying, could only think of my happiness after he was gone.

Flynn sits silently, not saying another word for a moment before standing. As he moves to leave, he reaches into his back pocket and pulls out a white envelope with my name on it.

"He also reminded me to give you this." Flynn hands me the envelope and turns to leave. "If you need anything today I'm only a phone call away." And with that, he makes his exit.

My mind is wild with imagination. What could this be? I don't have to wonder long as my body takes over and rips the folded side open. In Jack's own handwriting there is a letter along with what looks like an insurance policy for a large sum of money.

Dear Piper,

If you are reading this letter, then Flynn has had the unfortunate task of delivering it to you after my untimely death. As I write, I hope that I am writing this only for myself and that you will never see it. Nevertheless, I wanted to write it in case a day ever came that I must leave you.

My love, you have made my life worth living. You are the reason I got out of bed each morning and the reason I looked forward to going to bed each night. I am sorry that I will not be there to grow old with you and watch as we become the grumpy old couple we dreamed of becoming. I looked forward to being the ones who would sit on their porch, yelling at people as they walk by, complaining about ailments to strangers and laughing when they all give us dirty looks. I am sorry for not putting my clothes in the hamper and for forgetting milk even after you reminded me five times. Most of all I am sorry that I have left you alone. This will be the one regret of my life.

I thank you for being the best friend and wife a man could possibly have hoped to find. Thank you for letting me be a part of your life for as long as I could be.

I want you to be happy, I want you to smile, I want you to live. I know Casey and Abby will be there for you and will help push you to move on, but I want you to know that I want that more than anything else in the world.

Flynn will be there to help with the heavy lifting around the house, he will do it whether you want him to or not so just let him do it. Don't try to pay him, make him your marshmallow brownies and call it even.

I know moving on will be hard, but I want you to know this, I will always be a part of you and you a part of me. However, please do not let that hold you back from finding happiness again. I need you to be strong again for me, be strong for yourself, and strong enough to keep living... I will always love you.

From my heart to yours,

Jack

P.S. I didn't want you and Bryna to have to worry about anything so I took steps to make sure you will still be taken care of. Don't let the money change you, a million dollars isn't what it used to be... and watch out for those young hunky men just looking for a sugar mama.

I can hardly breathe when I'm finished reading. Had Abby come outside any later they may have found me on the ground dead in a puddle of my own tears. Abby, of course, runs to my side and starts to comfort me. She thinks this is *just* another burst of grief coming out, that is until I show her the letter.

Chapter Four

Anniversary

The sun beats on my face as my alarm clock rings loudly in my ear. I quickly reach over, slam my hand on the snooze button, and let out a small groan. It has been a year and three months since Jack died, and it still feels like it was yesterday.

Abby and Casey made plans to be here in an hour to pick me up. They have a *fun-filled, action-packed* day planned for us. This is their attempt at keeping my mind off what today is.

I love them for trying, but my second wedding anniversary without Jack is hardly something I can busy myself through. To tell you the truth, I actually just want to be alone today. Sleep in late, take a long hot bath, and then maybe grab a bite to eat at our favorite restaurant on my way to visit him. I say *him* as if I am in reality going to be able to see him, touch him, as I had done so many times before. Last year everyone had given me the space I needed and I am grateful for that, but since this year would have been our twentieth wedding anniversary, they insisted on taking me out.

Lying here letting my thoughts run wild with memories, I discover that as time has gone by the thought of not being able to touch him ever again doesn't throw me into a waterfall of emotions. Don't get me wrong, my heart still hurts for him, and I miss him with every aching bone in my body, but the tears are not trying to fight their way out of me as they once did.

Is a year all it takes to overcome the daily morning cry fest or have I just finally run out of tears? I take a deep breath and close my eyes for a moment so I can see him. I picture him across the table from me sporting his goofy little grin at some joke I made. He lifts the fork to take the last bite then leans over to kiss me, thanking me for a wonderful breakfast. The thought gives me what I needed, and have come to depend on as my new routine. A single tear escapes from my right eye, the warm liquid runs down my cheek and for that moment, I feel comforted.

I wipe the tear from my cheek and spring up from my bed. It is time to start this day and that means I actually need to shower. I would not say personal hygiene has become an issue, but I will say that my shampoo seems to be lasting a lot longer than it used to. I blame it on the morning *runs* I no longer take. Since I stopped my walks, I only feel the need to shower every other day, okay maybe I stretch it to every third day, four at the max if I have not left the house. Regardless of when I showered last, I most definitely need to shower today.

In thirty-two seemingly short minutes, I am showered, shaved, dried my hair, and even had time to put on my makeup. Casey and Abby should be here any minute. Casey and Abby have been showing up on average, twenty to thirty minutes early every time we have plans. I can't get too mad, everyone is still worried about me. I admit it annoyed me at first, although now I have grown to count on that extra little bit of time merely standing around chatting before I'm forced to leave my home to partake in some random activity that was planned in an effort to get me out of the house.

Casey and Abby have gotten to be nearly as bad a Bryna. After the funeral, she tried to tell me that she was going to drop out of school so she could move back home with me. I absolutely refused to let her when she continued to insist that she needed to be here for me and that school could wait. I assured her I would be fine and that Casey, Abby, and Flynn would be here to keep me from going crazy. When that didn't convince her, I pulled out the big guns and won the argument when I told her that her father would come haunt me if I allowed her to put off school. She chuckled, knowing that is exactly something her father would do. Although Jack was successful, he believed that had he gone to college, we would not have had such a rough start financially. He never actually regretted the choice he had to make about not going to college because he got Bryna instead. Jack knew he had gotten lucky in business and didn't want Bryna to have to rely on luck

I found out I was pregnant shortly after our high school graduation. We had always been so careful, we always used condoms, and I was on the pill. So when I missed my period I fell back on my, *it can never happen to me* way of thinking and I blew it off as some end of school stress causing the delay. However, when it still had not appeared in the two weeks that followed, I finally broke down and took a pregnancy test.

Positive, it was positive. How in the hell did this happen? What was I going to do? Was I ready to be a mom? Was Jack ready to be a dad? What were my parents going to say?

My brief jaunt down memory lane is interrupted by excessively peppy sounds coming from my front door.

"Hello... we're here," I hear Abby say as she walks through the threshold.

"Come on in, I am just getting ready to have a cup of coffee before we go," I yell back.

"Hurry it up. We have tons planned for today," Casey says in a hurried voice.

"Yeah, well you can sit your asses down and wait because you are the ones half an hour early. If I am going to be functional, I am going to need my coffee." I laugh, pouring the hot brown liquid into Jack's favorite old red coffee mug.

I never used to drink coffee. I actually hated the stuff, I always thought coffee tasted bitter and could never understand any one's need to drink it. Coffee had always been Jack's thing, though. He would not leave the house before he had at least one cup of the drink he called heaven in a glass. However, about a month after Jack passed, I found I missed the aroma of it wafting throughout the house. I started to brew a small pot each morning to feel like he was here with me. After about a week of pouring it down the drain each night, I felt bad for being so wasteful and started drinking it. Granted I added a ton of creamer to cut down on the actual flavor in the beginning. Today I am addicted to the stuff. I am fully convinced someone is adding crack to the beans and shipping it to unsuspecting caffeine seekers.

I take each sip slowly as the girls try to get me excited for the day with words like epic, unforgettable, and magical. I know they mean well, but they are hardly the ones I wanted to be spending today with. I fight the urge to slip into a fantasy where the last year and three months have all been but a bad dream and I wake up to Jack kissing my neck, wishing me a happy twentieth anniversary.

"Finally! Coffee is gone! Now it's time to get this party wagon on the road," Abby urges joyfully.

"Fine, fine, let's go," I say, carefully setting the mug in the sink and rolling my eyes at the enthusiasm.

"You are going to have so much fun today. We have so much planned," Casey informs me for the hundredth time.

"Guys, I told you I didn't want anything too over the top today," I lecture.

"Abby and I did not plan anything over the top, don't you worry," Casey assures me.

An hour later, we are pulling into a long driveway. Trees cover the road creating a what appeared to be a long tunnel. The light above tries its hardest to peek through the thick foliage, but for all its efforts it will have to wait for winter when the leaves have fallen from the trees to see what lies underneath.

At the end of the driveway, the trees open up to a large field with a single building in the middle surrounded by smaller trees and flower gardens. The small sign we pass says The Ando Spa and Resort.

"A spa? That is your bi
g idea of epic, unforgettable fun?" I mock.

"Nope, this is simply stop number one. We are getting a massage," Abby explains.

On any other day, I would love to be pampered like this, but today I do not feel the need to lie naked on some bed with some chick touching and rubbing on me, leaving my thoughts to run where they please. I want to be sitting on the riverbank next to *our* tree with a good book and a bottle of wine. Jack and I would often walk down to the riverbank near our house and have a day picnic. Jack would fish or try to fish anyway. He was never very good at it. I would sit back and read, looking up occasionally to watch him fight with the snag he cast his lure into. I do not know why he kept trying to fish, he never seemed to improve, but then I suppose that was part of his charm. He would never give up.

Pulling up to the big, ornately decorated front door, a young, handsome man with dark hair, tan skin, and wearing a white pajama-looking outfit comes running out to greet us.

"Good morning, ladies," he greets without the accent I had half expected to hear.

"Good morning," we all reply.

"Are we checking in or we are here for the day?" the man asks.

"Here for an hour or so, thank you," Casey instructs.

"Very good," he answers as he replaces Casey's keys with a valet card and proceeds to take care of parking for us.

Walking in the building, it is beautiful. The walls are covered in a gray stone with gold etchings along the ceiling. Plants are everywhere, making me feel like I traveled to the rain forest. I love the fresh scent that surrounds us. I can see why people come here to relax and I am regretting my earlier thoughts. This is where I want to be right now.

A woman dressed in the same white pajama outfit welcomes us as we approach the front desk.

"Welcome to the Ando Spa and Resort, how can I help you today?" she asks calmly.

"We have a reservation for massages today," Casey replies.

"Very good, let me get you checked in. May I please have your names?" the woman asks.

"Casey Nelson, Abby Reed, and Piper Reynolds," Casey tells her.

"I have you right here. I will let your masseurs know you are ready," she says and then walks back toward a frosted glass door.

"Masseur? Doesn't she mean masseuse?" I ask.

"Oh. Piper. You are in for such a treat. I found this place last year and it is... well you will see," Abby squeals.

"What kind of treat? What did you guys do?" I ask hesitantly, giving them the stink eye.

Before Abby can answer me, three men walk through the glass door, all dressed in the white pajama outfits and all extremely good looking. Okay, good looking is an understatement, these men are freaking gorgeous. We all seem to let out a small gasp as they walk toward us. I can feel my palms starting to sweat. Of all the things running through my head, my thoughts land on the possibility that my masseur will want to shake my hand, my now lightly damp hand. I quickly shove them into my pockets and squeeze the inner lining hoping that will help.

"Mrs. Reynolds?" hunk number one asks.

"Yes, that is me," I blurt. I feel my cheeks start to warm with the embarrassment of my excited tone. My God, I feel like a kid at Christmas waiting to open a giant gift that Santa left.

"My name is Toren, I will be your masseur today. Right this way please," he says, extending his arm toward the glass door.

"Whatever you say," I say as I step forward to follow him.

I look back to Casey and Abby and silently mouth the words *Oh My Gawd* to them. Casey and Abby have big shitty grins on their faces and give me a thumbs-up as I continue to follow Toren. I realized quickly that I should have been paying attention to where I was walking. As soon as I started to jokingly fan myself with my hand, I see Abby's expression change. She is trying to mouth something me, I can almost make out the words *watch out* when my body slams into the back of Toren.

"Oh shoot, I am so sorry," I say as I back away.

"Not a problem," he responds with a smirk.

My cheeks start to betray me by showing off the degree of my embarrassment, and my hands instinctively move to cover them, but it is too late. Everyone has seen the red glow emanating from them. You would think with as red as they have become that I was a thirty-something-year-old virgin about to get laid for the first time. Oh sure, everyone politely smiles, trying to comfort me from afar, but who are they kidding, I will never be able to live this down. I think my hand may have grazed his ass on top of it, his very tight ass I might add, and no doubt, Casey and Abby saw the whole freaking thing.

As we enter the low-lit massage room, Toren hands me a form attached to a clipboard to fill out, then asks that as soon as I am ready to go ahead and undress and lie face down on the sheet on the massage table. I feel my cheeks blush again. The thought of being naked in front of him after my inadvertent butt graze has my embarrassment reemerging. I am going to be under the sheet, I will still be naked, and he will be touching me. My face burns at that thought, I am sure my face is glowing like Rudolph's nose. Screw it, I am going to decide right now that I am going to suck it up and damn it I am going to enjoy this. The last year has been hell on my poor body, especially my shoulders. It is about time to get some of these knots worked out.

Chapter Five
Relaxed

One glorious hour later, Toren has finished working out my all knots, and I feel like melted butter. Before leaving the room, he tells me to take my time and to get up slowly when I am ready. Part of me doesn't ever want to leave this place. It is peaceful here, no one asking me how I am doing, looking at me, wondering what he or she should say if I spoke to them, or if they should say anything at all. You would have thought that after over a year that maybe, just maybe, people would have figured out how to have a normal conversation with me.

The soft music and the scent of jasmine still fill the air as I start to uncover myself from the warm blankets. My clothes tossed on a nearby chair are waiting for me to put them back on. Do I actually have to do anything more today? Can't this be enough? Jack and I never use to make a big deal about our anniversary so why should Casey and Abby feel the need to? I should admit, not making a big deal of our anniversary wasn't by choice. It was mostly because when we first got married we were new parents, young and so broke we couldn't even afford to put our two cents into a conversation. Jack was barely making over minimum wage working as a landscape technician, which was really just a fancy way of saying he cut grass, sprayed for weeds, and plowed snow in the winter. I worked odd retail jobs in the evenings so we could avoid daycare costs. I would like to say that after Jack and Flynn started Avery Reynolds Excavating & Landscape Services, and we became more financially stable, that we started making a bigger deal out of our special day, however, we were so used to doing something that didn't cost much that we never thought of doing anything more elaborate or costly to celebrate.

It had always been enough for just the two of us to take some time for each other. No elaborate gifts or fancy trips were needed, we were together and that is all that mattered.

I hear my cell phone vibrate and can tell by its special hum that it must be Abby urging me to hurry up. I think to myself, maybe if I tell them this took all my energy away, I can convince them to let me go home and relax in front of my television for the rest of the day. Doubtful.

I am pulling my shirt over my head when my phone buzzes yet again. I sit down on the chair to put my shoes on and reluctantly look at the screen.

ABBY: Hurry up time is a wasting!!!
ABBY: Don't make me come in there and get you!!!
ABBY: I will and you know it, get your ass out here!!!

I let out a loud sigh when I see her overuse of exclamation points, then start to type. It's a good thing Toren worked me over pretty good massaging me like I have never been massaged before or she might have gotten a different response from me, something I might have had to apologize for later.

ME: Keep your damn panties on... I thought this was my day, I will be out when I am good and ready.

After shoving my phone in my back pocket, I lean down to put my shoes on. When I sit up, I take one more deep breath, stand, and walk over to the door. I hesitate to open the door, but if I don't Abby will send a search party for me. I finally open the door and walk down the long white hallway back to the frosted door. I smile at Toren as he passes me, escorting his next client to another room. I can't help but wonder what could they possibly have planned next.

"It's about freaking time," Abby scolds me.

"Pipe down, this is a place of relaxation," I tell her with a snarky smirk.

"Whatever. Let's go, time's a wastin'. We got shit to do."

We pile back into the car, and it doesn't take long for us to start bragging about how awesome our massages were. Casey for some reason seemed unimpressed with hers. However, she is doing her best to play along. Abby will not shut up about how solid yet soft her guy's hands were, and how they worked her over like a two-dollar whore.

I smile at her comment, I can feel my mood lightening. I find that am starting to get excited about what is coming next.

"What is that smile about?" Casey asks.

"Nothing," I reply, acting as if I have no idea what she is talking about.

"No, not nothing. What is it?" she demands.

"Fine. I am thinking that I maybe, just maybe I might be glad you guys dragged me out of the house today."

"See I told you," Abby blurts as she gives Casey a playful nudge to her arm.

"Yeah, whatever, no need to rub it in," Casey replies.

"Now don't get too excited, I feel that way now, but I have no idea what else you have planned... I may hate you in an hour," I add playfully.

The car ride seems to fly by as we continue to gossip about random things. Okay, gossip might be a strong word. I haven't been out in the world enough since the funeral to have any real gossip. Yes, I left the house to do grocery shopping and tend to the legal matters the death of a loved one brings you. Then there were the nights that Casey and Abby dragged me to some movie or restaurant to entertain me.

Jack made sure I wouldn't have anything to worry about financially, and between the life insurance and the settlement her insurance company offered, Bryna and I will never have to worry about a thing as far as money goes. I still can't believe he had a letter attached to a million dollar life insurance policy ready and waiting should a day come that he would leave me unwillingly.

Jack had always been the breadwinner in our house. We decided early on that I would work as little as possible, and other than the few retail jobs I had at the beginning of our marriage, I haven't held a *real* job in years. Even after Bryna graduated, I didn't get a "real" job as others would call it. My job was to take care of the house and Jack. Of course, that didn't take eight hours a day so I volunteered at the local pet shelter.

A few weeks after the funeral, I started to resume my normal shifts at the shelter, but soon became overwhelmed with conversation about Jack and questions about how I was doing. I ended up telling the shelter I needed some more time off, and that I would call them when I was ready to start up again.

"We're here!" I hear Abby shout, as the car pulls into a spot in the mall parking lot.

"Shopping? Really?" I ask.

"Well, kind of," Casey tell me.

"Guys I *really* don't feel like shopping today."

"Don't worry, it's not real shopping," Abby tells me.

"I don't even feel like fake shopping."

"Just go with it," Casey adds with a smile and a nod.

I decide that if Casey is trying to convince me, it might

not be that bad… she knows better than to make me do something I am not in the mood to do. I give them one last look of warning, and they both smile and shake their heads yes before we exit the car and make our way to the mall entrance.

The mall is busy considering it is the middle of the week. Looking around, I see mostly moms with their kids doing what looks like some early back to school shopping. I bet the kids are thrilled. I actually kind of miss back to school shopping. I would save up for it so she wouldn't feel left out when she walked into those halls on her way to the next grade with all her friends in the latest fashions. Granted, she usually only got three or four new outfits, but it was enough to give her the extra little pep in her step the first few days. Before my memories fully take over, Casey pulls me back to reality.

"Okay, get ready for some more pampering," Casey says with a smile.

"Um, didn't we just leave a spa?" I ask, looking at the sign in front of me that reads Juarez Salon & Spa.

"Yes, but this is where we are getting our nails done, then our hair," Casey informs me.

"Are you kidding? Nails? When have you ever known me to get a manicure?" I ask laughing

"Never, and that is why we are doing manicure and pedicures today. Then we are going to do something with that hair of yours," Abby explains.

"And what is wrong with my hair?" I ask, giving my locks a comforting stroke.

"Nothing, we are simply going to give it a fresh look."

My joy of this news is overflowing. NOT. As much as I love to be all prettied up, I have always enjoyed doing it myself. I am not sure if this is because I had to for so many years or if I would have always liked doing it, but the idea of giving my hands and feet to a stranger to rub and then giving control of my hair over to a perfect stranger is pure madness.

Yes, I said madness.

"Come on, you will like it," Abby tells me and pulls at my arm leading me in.

The cute twenty-something girl sitting at the reception desk with her long brunette hair and dark smoky makeup done perfectly welcomes us and offers us a beverage before calling for our nail technicians. All I can think about is how happy I am that Bryna is not that type of girl. Don't get me wrong, I am sure this young lady is very sweet, but she seems like she would be extremely high maintenance.

The equally gorgeously made-up nail technicians lead us to the back of the spa for our pedicures. I have to admit that after getting a better look at these chairs I might have been missing out on something all these years. The chairs are black leather and large enough for two people to sit in. When I sit down in one, I quickly find they also come with some kind of remote control for you to change the massage levels and heat settings. This actually might not be that bad after all.

The hour and a half pass us by as if they were just minutes. Our hands and feet are scrubbed, full of lotion, polished, dried, and ready to go, for what I have no idea. It is worth mentioning that for my first ever professional manicure and pedicure it wasn't bad. It was enjoyable in a way that a girl could get used to that. We were all so busy talking and having a good time that Lindsey, my nail technician, didn't feel like a stranger for some reason.

Next we are whisked off to the salon where other long-legged beauties attempt to make something out of my long brown locks. I've never actually got into doing my hair in the latest fashion… In fact, I can't tell you the last time I used my blow dryer. Wait do I even own a blow dryer anymore? I'm sure I do, that and a three-inch curling iron that I have had for about fifteen years that I use maybe twice a year.

The two and half hours that it takes her to cut, color, and

style my hair, plus the forty-five minutes another woman spent putting makeup on me, is worth it when I look in the mirror and hardly recognize myself. My once dull brown hair is now a golden brown with hints of red shining through. My face is smooth looking with the blush highlighting my cheekbones. The eyes looking back at me are painted as if I'm going to go home and shoot porn. Okay, maybe not that bad, but to me it certainly looks unnatural.

As I continue to stare at myself, I start to think *if I tone it down a little I could actually get used to this look.*

"Hot mama," Abby says from behind me.

"I know, right? I think I could get used to this look," I joke.

"We have one last thing to do before we go home," Casey tells me.

"What? What could possibly be left on the list for today?" I ask.

"Well, it's only a pit stop."

"Guys, today has been amazing, but in truth, I am ready to go home and relax now," I say with a deep sigh.

"Come on, it is this one last stop and then home," Abby replies as she looks at her phone.

"Okay, but then we go back to my house for some comfy pants, pizza, and wine," I tell them.

I get no verbal response from either of them. Instead, I get two mischievous smirks. Rather than argue, I decide to keep my sanity intact and just smile, nod, and walk back out into the mall hallway while Casey stays back to pay.

Chapter Six
Dinner

After a "pit stop" at Macy's for Abby to run in and pick up a garment bag, we are *finally* on our way back to my house. I didn't bother to ask what was in the bag, no doubt it has to do with a master plan they have to get me out of the house again later tonight. There is no other logical conclusion I can come too, considering we have been pampered and prepped all day for a night out. I will truly hate to be the buzzkill after all they have done for me today, but I have had about enough of the running around. Don't get me wrong, I enjoyed myself today more than I ever thought I would, but it's time to sit back, drink wine, eat, and relax. Even if that means being all dolled up looking like we are supposed to be walking the red carpet watching some sappy romance.

On our way home, I tried to get them to stop for pizza. I was told to stop being a backseat driver and not to worry about food. I eventually gave up and protested with a silent pout.

When we pull up to the house, I see Flynn's car parked in

the driveway. I almost blurt out a question of what he is doing here but remember he mentioned he was going to stop by today or tomorrow to take a look at the clothes dryer for me. It seems like it is taking longer and longer to dry my clothes. I was going to go buy a new one. However, Flynn insisted on taking a look at it for me first.

"Oh look, Flynn is here?" Abby questions in a fake *I'm going to pretend I didn't know he was here* tone.

Casey quickly shoots an evil look at her that has my curiosity level at a ten. Before I can question her odd tone, the car is in park and they each jump out of the car as if it was on fire.

I give the now empty car a questioning look before grabbing my purse and also exiting. Completing their marathon sprint, they are both already at the front door waiting for me as I close the car door behind me.

"You guys are up to something. What's going on?" I ask.

"Nothing, why do you ask?" Abby says with a big grin on her face.

Casey gives her another evil glare before turning away to avoid eye contact with me.

"Well, you seem to have known Flynn would be here. On top of that, it's not even dark out yet and my drapes are all closed," I point out.

"Nothing, don't spoil it. You will find out soon enough. Now, when we get in please let us take you right up to your room, no looking around," Casey pleads.

"Guys *really*, no more surprises. I only want to sit back and relax for the rest of the night," I beg.

"Don't worry, it's nothing big, it's just…" Abby starts before Casey punches her in the arm.

"OUCH! You didn't have to hit me that hard," she cries.

"Yes, yes I did. Now stop talking before I tape your damn mouth shut," Casey hissed as she opens my front door.

I shake my head and follow Casey through the threshold. Abby promptly follows behind me, tossing her arms up to cover my eyes, then races me upstairs to my bedroom.

I hear the bedroom door close and Abby's hands fall from my face. The garment bag I saw Casey had draped over her arm while standing on the porch is now lying open on the bed.

It is a beautiful black dress with a strapless top and chiffon skirt with a beautiful rhinestone belt. It reminds me a little of a severely upgraded version of the dress from *Dirty Dancing* that Baby wore in the last scene. It is the most beautiful dress I have ever seen. Ever since I first saw the movie, I have always wanted a dress like this. The way the skirt flowed on Jennifer Grey making her look so graceful, so beautiful, I couldn't help wanting to be her, to have Patrick Swayze dancing like that with me. I knew I could never be her so I soon wanted to at least own a dress like that so I could be that beautiful.

I slowly pick it up carefully from the bed, treating it like a newborn child rather than the yards of fabric that it is. I walk to the full-length mirror and hold it up to me to get a better look.

"Do you like it?" Casey asks with a large smile on her face.

"Holy shit you guys! You did not have to do this... this is way too much... this dress had to be two hundred dollars," I scold.

"Actually closer to three," Abby blurts, prompting another punch from Casey.

"No, you can't do this. You need to take it back," I demand.

I unwillingly pull it away from my body in an effort to put it back in its protective bag, knowing I cannot accept this gift.

"It's nonreturnable, it was a custom made for you," Casey informs me as she crosses her arms with a look of satisfaction.

"Liar. Macy's doesn't do custom pieces."

"Not normally no, but they do alterations and this was in a way an alteration. It started off as two dresses and now it is one. Therefore, you have no choice but to keep it."

"Guys, really this is way too much," I say as quickly.

"It's yours now, and if you feel that strongly about it, you can give it to some woman at the homeless shelter." Casey jokes.

I pick the dress back up and walk across the room to the mirror to admire it once again with a large smile on my face. Holding the dress up to myself, I move my hips from side to side, watching the loose chiffon flow back and forth.

"Come on, put it on already," Abby demands.

Twisting of my arm would not be necessary. I did wholeheartedly love the dress and since they did go through so much trouble to have it made for me it was my absolute duty as the gift recipient to at least try it on for them. I wouldn't want to offend my friends after all.

I rip off my clothes and slip the dress on. The chiffon feels so soft against my skin that I briefly wonder why all clothing isn't made of chiffon. After a little help with the zipper, I step once again in front of the mirror to admire the masterpiece in the reflection.

I have a hard time believing it is me looking back, my hair, makeup, this dress makes me feel like someone else entirely. I can't help but run my fingertips over the smooth fabric now hugging my skin. The feeling is heavenly.

"Don't forget the shoes," Casey says as she pulls them out of the bottom of the garment bag.

My heart stops once more at these magnificent creations. I look to see black glittered four-inch shoes with silver glitter heels. As I slip them on my feet, I feel like a princess getting ready for the ball. My only wish is that my lost prince would be there to greet me at the bottom of the staircase.

"You look incredible!" Abby tells me.

"Beautiful, you are simply beautiful," Casey agrees as she hides her tears.

"You guys, today has been amazing. I... I... I have no words," I stutter as I fight the tears of joy trying to come out and ruin my makeup.

I continue to admire myself in the mirror as Abby and Casey change into dresses they had in a bag I hadn't noticed hidden under the garment bag when we came into the house.

"Okay, let's head downstairs. I think someone is waiting for us," Abby says with excitement.

Casey opens the bedroom door and I see red and white rose petals have been laid down on the floor in a path meant for us to follow. As follow the path down the stairwell and into the living room, my jaw drops when I see the dining room filled with more red and white roses, alongside the many lit candles that give off an enchanting glow.

Flynn and Bryna are standing near the head of the table that is set for six with new china I have never seen before and a centerpiece made up of a single gift wrapped in white paper surround by red roses and candles.

"Happy Anniversary, Mom," Bryna says, pulling me out of my shock.

"Bryna, what are you doing here? Did you and Flynn, did you do all this?" I ask, grabbing at my heart that is about to explode in my chest.

"Flynn picked me up this morning and brought me home. We did, but we may have had a little help. Do you like it?" she responds.

"No, I love it. And to think I wanted to be alone today."

"Mom, there was no way we were going to let you be alone today," Bryna says as she walks to me and gives me the biggest hug I have ever gotten.

"Come on. Sit down and let's eat," she tells me.

"Wait, aren't Dave, Chuck, and Leo going to join us?" I ask.

"No, Dave had to work late again," Abby tells me.

"And Chuck had to drive Leo to football camp."

"I can't believe Leo is going to be a freshman this year."

I smile.

"I know, what happened? I blinked and he was no longer my little baby boy."

Bryna leads me to my seat and when I see the setting next to mine has a single red rose on the silver lined plate I think of Jack. He would have found this cheesy and over the top. He was never a romantic kind of guy. He did the flower thing and a nice massage or midnight candlelight bath from time to time, but something like this, he would say something like, *Why on earth would I spend all that money to get laid? That is just a legal form of prostitution. You know deep down that if the guy does all that crap, he is only doing it to get some tail,* and then laugh hysterically at his own ridiculously stupid joke.

Once everyone is seated, Flynn picks up a small bell I hadn't noticed and rings it. As he sets it down, five men come walking out of the kitchen in a line wearing perfectly pleated black pants, white jacket uniforms, and white gloves. Each one of them takes a position behind one of us and all at once, they place a plate in front of us on the table then immediately retreat back to the kitchen without saying a word. A soft melody starts to play and I realize it is to be our dinner music.

The fruit that has been placed in front of us looks like a magnificent work of sculpted art rather than something we are supposed to destroy by eating. A small apple cut and shaped to be a swan was in the center of the plate with five watermelon bites in the shape of roses surrounding the swan. The fine details are unbelievable. If I could, I would put this plate on a shelf and admire them for years to come.

"Aren't you going to eat?" Casey asks,

"No, they are too beautiful to eat. I think we are just supposed to look at them," I reply, laughing.

They each look to one another, smiling. They all seem to be very proud of my reaction.

"Come on. You will piss the chef off of you don't,"

Flynn adds as he takes a bite of the swan's head, smiling.

After we all chuckle as his boyish actions, I finally manage to convince myself to take the wing of the swan and place the thin slice of apple on my tongue. My taste buds scream with excitement. The flavor is indescribable, so sweet and crisp. You would think this was the first time I had ever tried an apple with the way my taste buds were now craving another bite.

Now that the shock of everything is starting to wear off, I feel more comfortable and conversation begins to fill the air. Including telling me that this will be a full six-course meal and not to over stuff myself on any one dish.

We go on to tell Flynn and Bryna about our day and they relive their excitement of planning and getting set up for today.

Meanwhile, we continued to be served by our seemingly invisible wait staff. If it weren't for our empty plates being taken and replaced with the next course, you would never know any of them were there. Even when you did interrupt your conversation to thank them again and again, they would only nod and smile.

Appetizers are now laid out in front of us and are absolutely mouthwatering. The chicken wrapped in bacon covered with a maple glaze next to potatoes that have been thinly sliced and lightly topped with cheese, bacon, chives, and sour cream are begging for me to eat them.

Before we know it, our plates are replaced with the next course—salad. The salad is not disappointing, small by design it is the best-looking cranberry walnut salad I have ever seen.

"There is no way I'm going to be able to keep eating," I say while shoving the last bite of salad in my mouth.

"I know this is amazing. I don't ever want this to end," Bryna replies.

"Flynn, you truly outdid any expectation we had when you brought this crazy plan to us," Casey says while raising her wine filled glass.

"Flynn? This was all your idea?" I ask.

"Well, not entirely... I will explain after dinner. Right now I want you just to sit back and enjoy," he replies.

I smile in agreement, deciding not to push him to explain everything right now. However, when I see Bryna has a funny grin on her face that is so cheesy, that pretty much screams this was her idea and she has something else up her sleeve.

The rest of dinner was equally amazing. The pineapple mint sherbet for our palate cleanser, the roasted duck with orange sauce for the main course, and the white chocolate raspberry cheesecake bites for dessert were truly heaven in my mouth.

When the chef finally exits from the kitchen to greet us, we stand and give him a round of applause. He takes his bow. The waiters once again return with yet another for each of us with three small tarts on them. One coconut cream, one passion fruit raspberry, and the last he called a stone fruit tart. They are his thank you to us for having him in our home. He was nice enough to pose for a picture with all of us and then retreated to the kitchen to finish cleaning up.

As we retire to the living room, the wait staff finishes clearing the remaining plates and glasses from the table then disappear into the kitchen for the final time.

I cannot help but to pay attention to the fullness of my belly. I probably gained twenty pounds tonight, and every pound was more than worth it. My taste buds have been teased and pleasured with so many wonderful things I think eating anything less than gourmet meals from this point on will feel like an unprovoked punishment for the poor little things.

Chapter Seven
The Gift

Taking a seat on the couch next to Bryna, I see the joy in her eyes. I see the same joy in everyone's eyes as I look to each of them with a smile.

"I am so full. I don't think I will need to eat for a month," Abby blurts as she falls into the loveseat across from me.

"So, we are going to do this every night from now on right?" I joke.

"Sure, I think we could all get used to this kind of treatment," Casey adds.

"Yeah, but then we would have to build a gym in the basement to counter the five million calories we just ate," Abby states, laughing.

Abby is the health nut among us, always trying to make sure we make healthy choices. She obviously tossed that mentality out the window for tonight.

"Okay, can we give it to her now?" Bryna blurts suddenly.

"I think we have to before she passes out into a food coma," Flynn acknowledged.

Bryna does an excited bounce and claps before she jumps up to retrieve the small gift that made up the centerpiece on the table.

"Oh, no, no, really… no more gifts. You have all done so much for me today and spent so much money that I cannot accept any more gifts," I declare as Bryna comes running back into the living room and places the gift in front of me on the coffee table.

"Whatever, Mom. You deserve all of this and more. Besides it's not from us," she responds with a smile.

"Then who is it from?" I ask, looking at them for someone to answer.

"You will just have to open it to find out," Casey tells me.

I give each of them a confused look before turning my attention to the gift in front of me calling for the wrapping to be ripped away to reveal the answer to my lingering question.

My heart races as I scoot forward on my seat to reach for the perfectly wrapped gift, the white paper with a silver bow staring back at me with the secret they hold.

The excitement takes over and before I can calm myself, I grab the folded corner on the end and I rip open the package to reveal an envelope and a rectangle jewelry box.

My heart almost stops when I see the handwriting on the front of the envelope. This is not possible. Why would there be an envelope with my name on it written in Jack's handwriting?

"What the hell is this?" I demand.

The smiles that filled everyone's faces are now fading.

"This is not funny, what the hell were you guys thinking?" I demand again.

"No, Mom, will you please open it already?" Bryna begs, moving closer to me.

I reluctantly reach for the letter and open it. In the envelope, there are two pieces of paper, one a plain white paper and the second a piece of what looks like old notebook paper. As I unfold the first one, the top paper looks like a letter from Jack. I give everyone another evil glare. I'm sure they meant well and how they were able to make it look like Jack's handwriting I have no idea, but this was crossing a huge line. Why they thought this would be okay, I cannot begin to imagine. My eyes turn back to the letter and begin to read what it has to say.

Piper,

Today we have been married for twenty years. It has been such a journey for us and I have loved each and every day.

Although we may have our happiness with each other, I know that the start of this marriage was not what either of us had planned. We had plans to go to college, travel, experience life the best we could before saying I do and starting a family.

That being said I would not change a thing, I have had you in my arms for twenty years as my wife, and you gave me the most beautiful daughter.

You have given me so much and never asked for anything in return that I wanted to do something special for you.

My gift to you is Carpe Diem. What do I mean by that you are wondering and probably giving me a "you're crazy" look right now, but it is just that, Carpe Diem.

The next paper you open you will find your high school Carpe Diem list. You have been so busy taking care of us that you never had time to cross anything off the list, once upon a time you were hell bent on adding to your list and crossing items off to make sure that you made the most of each day.

So for the next year, we are going to cross some things off your list and have some of the adventures we had to put on hold.

From my heart to yours,

Jack

My hands start to shake and I can feel my heart trying to escape from my chest. I can barely breathe deep enough to form any words.

"Mom, are you alright?"

I look at her with tear-filled eyes.

"How… I…" I stutter.

Flynn stands and walks toward me. He takes a seat next to me and reaches for my hand.

"Piper, Jack had been planning your twentieth anniversary for years. He had it all planned out on what he wanted tonight to be and looked forward to it. I didn't think he would want you to miss out on all his hard work and since I have been hearing about every last detail for years, I called everyone to see what they all thought about helping Jack out one last time and giving you the gift he wanted you to have," Flynn explains.

Casey and Abby have tears running down their faces when I look to them for confirmation. They each nod and then I look to Bryna.

"When Flynn called me and told me about Dads plan I knew we had to do this, we had to do it for you and for Dad. He would have wanted us to," Bryna adds

I say nothing as I reach for the second piece of paper that is still folded. The paper feels worn and the creases are weak from being opened and closed many times. As I unfold it, I see Carpe Diem written at the top in large letters, below that my name Piper Allen and the date February 23rd.

It was an old school assignment, I recognize it as the one that I had to do in high school English class my senior year.

My teacher, Mrs. Jenkins, was out sick and we had a substitute teacher, Mrs. Foster. She was kind of a hippy-looking woman. She wore a long flowing skirt and a loose-fitting top. The guys in the class were having a blast secretly trying to figure out if she was wearing a bra.

Since Mrs. Jenkins had recently finished our lesson on poetry and had not started the next lesson, Mrs. Foster decided to make it a fun day. She started talking to us about some experiences she had. One of the other students made comments about a bucket list and one thing led to another, and the next thing you know, she was lecturing us about the difference between her experiences and a bucket list.

"A bucket list is filled with all the things you hope you can do one day and honestly probably will not have the chance to do. I live each day as if it is my last and choose to seize every opportunity," she told us.

Most of the class gave her a look of not caring so she took it to the next step.

"Who here has heard the phrase Carpe Diem?" she asked.

We responded with silence, that is until one of the idiot football jocks shouted, "This is English class, not French class," throwing several other students alongside him into a fit of laughter.

"It's Latin, smart-ass. It means 'seize the day,' taken from the Roman poet Horace's *Odes*, and that will become today's assignment," she stated.

The laughter was replaced with a sigh of disappointment that quickly spread through everyone in class, everyone but me that is. I was intrigued by the stories she told us and although they were not all filled with travels to distant lands, each one was inspiring in its own way. To think that by looking around your own community, you could create your own adventure.

"Okay here is your assignment. For the next twenty minutes, I want you all to make a list, a Carpe Diem list. It should be a list of things you can do to seize the day and make it special. It can be as simple as taking a walk in the park, to traveling, but each item must all be things that you feel you would be able to reasonably do without a large bank account."

I loved this assignment. It was one of the best ones I had been given. A road map to making our own adventures rather than waiting for them to happen to us.

Bryna pulls me back from my memories when she touches my shoulder and leans down to read my list. I look around in awe. All of this was Jack. Jack had all this planned for me and my friends, my family carried out his plan.

The pampering, the dinner, and this wonderful, thoughtful gift.

As Bryna finishes reading the list, Flynn grabs my attention when he reaches for the rectangular jewelry box I had forgotten about.

"I think you will find that you will need this," he says, handing me the black velvet box.

I reach for the small box and open it slowly. My eyes tear up again when I see a black and silver ballpoint pen.

"I think you will find you can cross another one off your list," he adds.

I take a closer look at my list for the first time in over twenty years and read carefully, looking for the item I remember so vividly writing down.

Get a tattoo

~~Work at a haunted house~~

Create a secret family recipe

Fun with Girlfriends

Fall asleep under the stars

Learn to Ski

Try Golfing

Complete 25 acts of kindness

Make a difference in someone life

Carpe Diem

Take a picture in the same spot in each season
Have a whipped cream fight
Eat dinner and go to a movie by myself
Learn how to shoot a gun
Learn to dance
Slow dance in the rain
Skydive
Take a cooking class
~~Fall in love~~
Marry my best friend
Go on a no limit-shopping spree
Ride in a helicopter
Have a silly day
Write something in wet cement
Have a full moon party
Go skinny-dipping
~~Do a polar plunge~~
Go somewhere tropical
~~Win a contest~~
~~Volunteer my time~~
Watch the sun go down and the stars come out
Learn to knit
Go camping
Have my palm read
Create a board game
Go apple picking
Plant a garden
Take a canoe Trip
~~Take a walk with my mom~~
~~Go fishing with my dad~~
Eat a six-course meal

As I get to the end of my list, I find the item I am looking for and carefully draw a line through it.

~~Eat a six-course meal~~

Casey and Abby eventually say their good-nights and head home. Bryna heads up to her old room to head to bed. I was not nearly ready for bed, I was still sipping on some coffee, thinking about the evening. After tonight, I need to feel a little bit more of Jack with me so I brewed a small pot, and grabbed Jack's favorite red coffee cup from the shelf. I pour a second glass for Flynn, and we move our conversation to the front porch.

"You don't have to stay. I'm sure you are tired," I say, taking a seat.

"No, I'm fine… I think I am still coming off the adrenaline of the day."

"Flynn, you did an amazing job. Jack would be truly proud of everything you were able to pull off today."

"I can't take any of the credit, it was all his idea. He would go on and on about every little detail he could think of and wrote it all down in his 'anniversary journal' he kept at the office," he replies, smirking.

I could tell he was reliving some of the conversations he had shared with Jack, as his smirk turned into a large smile and then a small chuckle.

"I can't tell you how much this means to me, but I can't ask you to foot the bill for Jack's master plan. Tell me the amount and I will write you a check," I offer.

"Ha, let me think about that. Ah, no. I don't think so. And even if it was my money I used, I wouldn't have let you pay me back." Flynn chuckles.

"I don't understand, whose money did you use?"

"Jack's. He had been saving for this for years, doing odd jobs for extra cash in the beginning and then having payroll process two checks for him so you would never know he was skimming."

"He did?" I ask.

"Yep, made me promise never to tell you no matter how broke you were at times."

"I can't believe he did that. Wait when did he work these side jobs?"

"Well, do you remember all those times he and I would hang out at my house for football, or helping me with some lame project, or the time he and I went on our fishing trip without his tackle box?"

"Yes…"

"He was off doing jobs. You almost caught us once in a lie, and Jack was convinced you were going to think he was cheating on you."

"Oh my God, yes, I knew you were lying," I blurt, laughing, knowing exactly the memory he was referring to.

It was about ten years ago, Jack and Flynn had made plans to go canoeing and camping for a boys' weekend. It was supposed to be a cheap weekend away. After Jack got home, he was limited on his excitement to tell me about the weekend and then two weeks later when I got our visa bill it showed a charge for the River's Edge Motel. When I asked Jack about it, he said that Flynn met some girl at the bar they stopped at along the river and Flynn hooked up with her. Jack claimed that Flynn didn't have his wallet on him so he gave Flynn our credit card and that he would pay us back.

The story did not make sense to me since Flynn had been kind of dating someone at the time and Flynn didn't seem the type to cheat. I was a little suspicious until later that day Flynn popped by with the amount of the charge and gave it to Jack. I walked in on the conversation and asked what was going on. When Flynn blushed at my question and told me he owed Jack some money, I believed the story

"That was a flat out lie. I never hooked up with a chick that weekend, I wasn't even there. He rented a motel room for an out of town job and used the wrong credit card to pay for it," Flynn explains.

"I can't believe that is the story he came up with," I reply, smiling.

"No kidding, I was pretty pissed. I, of course, played along so he wouldn't blow his cover."

"I suppose that clears that up, and I'm so glad that you didn't hook-up with a random chick. I actually thought less of you after I heard that."

"I know, I could see it in your eye when you looked at me that day," he says as he takes his last sip of wine avoiding eye contact.

"So, are you going to let me in on the rest of Jack's plan?" I ask, bringing the conversation back to something a little more comfortable.

"Nope."

"No? Why not."

"Because he wanted it all to play out a certain way and I'm going to do my best to help him with that."

"Okay, so then what was his next step?"

"I'm not going to give you any details yet, I will give you some warning when the next item is coming," Flynn says and then pauses for a moment

He is holding something back or trying to figure out how to tell me something. I can see the struggle he is fighting with himself and I want to help, but how can I when I don't know what it is.

"The plan wasn't fully complete," he tells me.

"That's okay, I..." I start to say before he interrupts me.

"I know, but I should warn you, I have a few of the letters he had already written. I wanted to warn you because I still plan to give them to you when the time is right," he explains

I sit quietly, looking at him for more, but he doesn't speak. He is sitting quietly playing with the empty coffee cup.

"Thank you," I finally say.

"I thought after your reaction to the letter tonight I should warn you."

"Yes, it was a bit of a shock. I never in a million years

would have expected this from him. He never was into that mushy gushy romance stuff."

"He loved you so much that he would have done anything for you."

Rae Matthews

Chapter Eight
The Adventure Begins

My dreams are slowly pulled from me when I hear someone calling my name. I try to hold on tight to the random dream I can no longer recall.

"Piper, oooooh Piper," I hear whispering in my ear.

"What?" I reply with my face buried in my pillow.

"It's morning!"

I glance over at the clock and see the numbers 7:16 a.m. staring back at me. I roll my eyes and push my face back into the warmth of the down feathers that cradle my head so perfectly.

"Come on! Don't you want to know what we are doing today?" Abby says while cuddling up next to me, stroking my hair.

"No, I want to go back to bed. You kept me up until all hours of the night, remember?"

"Oh come on, it was *not* that late." She laughs.

"I think you are mistaken my dear, it was at least one twenty-five a.m. the last time I looked at the clock," I remind her.

"Come on, I will start some coffee. Flynn will be here soon to give us the deets."

"If by soon you mean two hours," I yell to her as she leaves my bedroom.

"Yeah, well we need time to get ready," she says peeking back around the wall.

"I love Abby, I love Abby, I will not strangle Abby, Abby is my friend, I will not kill her," I quietly chant to myself.

My eyes are pretty pissed off at me right now and would really, really like me to let them close again so that I can fall back into the peaceful sleep I was enjoying. However, Abby is right, I do need to get up so we have time to shower and get ready.

My brain is starting to wake up and the excitement I felt last night when Flynn called to tell me that he will be stopping by at nine o'clock in the morning to pick me up for one of my Carpe Diem items. As soon as he said the words, my heart started to race and I could not stop the smile from forming on my face.

I, of course, asked for details, but he was a brick wall. I got nothing out of him, other than Casey would not be coming and that it would be only Abby and him joining me on this one.

The last month waiting and waiting to find out when and what I would be doing next has been extremely annoying. No one would tell me anything and Flynn was the worst, he kept insisting that this was all part of Jack's plan and that I would find out only when it was time. I joked that I doubt it was Jack's plan to end up in divorce court because toying with me like this may have done just that.

I have to admit I was impressed with Abby, even when I called Abby to come over to calm my nerves, she didn't crack under the pressure, or the three bottles of wine, or the half-asleep interrogation I tried on her. Nothing, nada, el zippo... this makes me think she has no idea what we are doing but wants me to think she does.

I wish Bryna had come home for summer break. I might have been able to pull some information from her. Unfortunately, for me, she is a good girl who listens to her mother. After a good lecture from me about going on and living her life and not worrying about me, she decided to actually listen to me and stayed living with her friends and got a job there for the summer.

"Coffee is ready, get your ass down here," Abby yells at me from downstairs.

"Coming, Mother," I shout back at her.

"Don't make me come up there and get you," she yells, laughing.

Now that I am fully awake and it is getting closer to getting my answers, my tummy is fluttering with excitement. I jump out of bed and run toward the stairs, my feet quickly taking each step as it has done a thousand times before.

Turning the corner, I see Abby leaning on the kitchen island, coffee in hand with a smirk on her face. Jack's red coffee mug is across from her, steaming with the freakily brewed brown liquid heaven waiting for me.

"Happy twenty years and one month anniversary," she tells me.

"That is the dumbest thing I have ever heard, but thank you," I reply.

As I approach the cup, I see that it is sitting on top of an envelope with my name scribbled in Jack's handwriting.

"You asshole! Did you have that letter all night?" I demand, reaching across the island to give her a friend-punch to the bicep.

"Ouch, yes! You didn't have to hit me so hard," she says, laughing and rubbing her arm.

"Oh my God, I hate you. Why didn't you let me have it last night?"

"Because that is was not part of the plan... The plan was for you to find it with your coffee."

"How in the hell did you not break last night? I was determined to get information out of you."

"For one, Flynn prepped me, and two, I have no idea what we are doing today. My job was to place the letter."

"But how did he know I would call and invite you over last night."

"Really? Why would he make it a point to tell you Casey isn't coming and that I was?"

"Touché."

"Okay, now open the damn letter. It has been a small slice of hell having and not being able to open it."

I give her a dirty little look and finally pick up the envelope, rip open the side and pull out the letter.

Good morning Beautiful,

I hope you are ready for some fun, I probably should have picked an easier adventure, from your list, but I have to try to top last month... so put on some comfortable clothes, grab your tennis shoes and a hair thingy because baby, we are going skydiving today. That's right, go big or go home, we are gonna jump out of a plane at 14,000 feet.

Why you ask? Well, you are the one that put this idiotic, insane thing on your list so ask yourself. So stop giving me that look and go get ready so we can go risk our lives for an amazing adrenaline rush.

Jack

P.S. you might want to bring an extra pair of panties, you know just in case.

Has he lost his freaking mind? Jump out of a plane? Why would he think I would still want to do that at this age? Sure, when I was eighteen it sounded like a great idea. Not at freaking thirty-nine.

"Come on, are you going to tell me?" Abby begs.

"Yeah, um I think Jack was going crazy?" I respond in disbelief.

"Why, what are we doing?" Abby asks again.

When I don't answer her, she runs around the island to read the letter for herself. I don't stop her as she grabs the letter and begins to read it. I pick up the red mug to let the warm liquid comfort me as I watch her excitement grow.

"Hell yeah! I have always wanted to skydive," Abby suddenly shouts out.

"Are you batshit crazy?"

"Hey, it's on *your* list don't blame me."

"I wanted to do it when I was eighteen, not now. No, we need to call Flynn to change it, we can do something else today."

"Good luck with that one."

"This is my gift and if I want to exchange it, I can." I laugh.

"Sure you can, just like Jack would have let you *exchange* it."

I look at Abby and know she is right. Jack never would have let me exchange it for another item on my list. He worked so hard on planning everything that he would have found a way to talk me into it.

I take my last sip of coffee, hold out the red mug, and whisper a few words to Jack.

"Fine, have it your way, I will go jump out of a plane and you can sit up on your cloud and laugh all you want, but when I see you again, you better watch out 'cause I am going to kick your angel ass."

I look over my shoulder to see that Abby is not paying attention to my madness then whisper one last thing, "I love you, and I love that you did this, I just wish you were here with me." I kiss the cup and set it back on the island.

I know, I know. Who in their right mind kisses a cup as if it is their dead husband? I guess that would be me... He used that cup so much and it was his absolute favorite. He said it fit perfectly in his hand and didn't get too hot when the coffee was poured into it.

An hour later, Flynn is walking into the kitchen and has a goofy-looking smile on his face. He knows me too well and knows how I must have reacted to the letter. In fact, he doesn't bother to ask after Abby gives him a smile and a nod. I hate them. They are loving every minute of this.

"Okay ready?" Flynn finally asks.

"You really couldn't have made any changes to his plan?" I blurt.

"Nope."

"Whatever... let's get this over with. And if I die today you guys better hope I don't come back and haunt you," I say.

"Oh come on, deep down inside your inner child is screaming with excitement," Abby says.

Abby might be a little bit right, thinking about jumping from a plane for the last hour brought back all the feelings I had about it the day I wrote it on the list. The idea of losing all control and letting gravity take over is an exciting idea.

Abby and Flynn turn to leave as I pick up the red coffee cup to put it in the sink and that is when the unthinkable happens. Why, why did I have to pick up the cup right now, why couldn't I have left it where it was and clean it up later, why had I set my purse next to my feet, why, why, why? Those questions ran through my head as I tripped on my purse precisely enough for me to lose my grip on the coffee mug. Jack's favorite red coffee mug. My body moves quickly, flailing about making a valiant effort to save the red cup from its fate.

"Nooooooo," I scream.

Flynn and Abby turn around just in time to see me and

the red cup on the floor, my finger only inches away from being able to save the one thing that makes me feel like a piece of Jack is still with me.

"Piper! Are you okay? What happened?" Abby says as she runs to my side.

"Jack's coffee cup..."

We all take a moment to examine the shattered pieces that used to be Jack's favorite coffee cup. The cup that he would use every morning at our breakfast—it's weird, I'm not quite sure where he got the cup from. It was the only one we had that looked like that and he has had it for as long as I can remember.

"Piper, I am so sorry," Abby says, breaking the silence.

"My heart feels as it has broken all over again. I know it is *just* a cup, but..."

"I know," she says, interrupting me.

"I knew the cup wouldn't last forever, I foolishly hoped it would," I say, wiping a tear from my eye.

"Maybe we can glue it back together. The pieces look big enough," Abby says as she picks up a few of the pieces and tries to twist and turn the edges to make it fit back together.

"It's okay, let's just go. I will clean this up later."

"Are you sure? We can clean it up for you," Flynn asked.

"No, thank you, I will do it later. I know it's strange, but I want to do it myself and I don't want to do it right now," I reply.

They each nod as I pick myself up off the ground, brush-off my jeans, then pick up my purse and with my head held high, I make my way to the front door.

"Let's do this!"

Rae Matthews

Chapter Nine
The Sky is The Limit

The drive was not as long as I thought it was going to be. Don't get me wrong, two hours is still a long ride, however after the morning I had, I truly thought it would feel longer with the anticipation that has been growing. Flynn and Abby did a great job at redirecting my attention to what we were about to do and building back up my excitement.

Turning down the road, we are greeted by the sight of three parachutes floating down with the blue sky above them. For those few, their adventure is coming to an end as ours is only beginning.

When we finally pull up to the small airport, it was not what I expected. Granted I'm not actually sure what I was expecting, it's not like I have any experience with this. The parking lot is covered with gravel and behind the sign that reads "Skydivers check in at hangar number two." You can see four small plane hangars.

My heart is pounding and my stomach is alive with the excitement. Are we actually going through with this? Are we truly dumb enough to jump out of a plane where our only chance of survival is the skill of the person attached to us.

All three of us have smiles on our faces as we exit the car and silently follow the path that leads us to hangar number two. As we approach the hangar, there is a small door propped open with a sign that says Drop Zone Skydiving Inc. It's not anything special, but it works.

As we enter the hangar, we see several employees to our left repacking parachutes behind a rope line. A small waiting area with couches faces a television currently playing a video of people jumping. To our right, there is a small plane also behind a rope line, and in front of us there is an office with a small window, the sign next to it says registration.

"Here we go, no turning back now," Abby says and does a hop skip right for the window.

"I think you are a little too eager to die." I laugh.

"Die, who's going to die?"

The strong Australian accent coming from behind me startles me. As I turn to look, I see a gorgeous, tall, dark-haired Aussie with dark eyes staring back at me. My heart skips when he smiles and winks at me then turns to go about his business. I watch him walk away until Flynn whispers in my ear.

"I'm sure he would be happy to show you a thing or two."

"I have no idea what you're talking about you pervert." I smile.

"What? I'm talking about skydiving. I'm sure he would be happy to show you how to skydive... What did you think I was talking about?"

"Yeah right."

"I think someone needs to get her mind out of the gutter."

I give him a playful shove and walk over to join Abby in line for registration. She is up next and is as giddy as a little kid at Christmas. As Flynn and I approach Abby, the woman behind the window welcomes us and hands us each a clipboard. She asks us to fill out the attached paperwork and when we bring it back she will need to see our driver's license.

The waivers seem to be pretty basic. If you die it's not our fault and no one can sue us. If you are injured it is not our fault and you cannot sue us. You understand by signing this document that you are participating in an extreme sport that could result in your death. Then it asks for emergency contact information in case of injury or death.

I look at the last line again. Who do I want them to call in case I die? I don't want them to call Bryna, I'm not sure she would be able to handle that. My parents would have a heart attack at the thought of me falling from a plane to my death so I suppose I should put down Casey since she is the only person left that would understand what in the world am I doing jumping from a plane. I finish filling out the rest of the form and sign my name. I open my purse and reach for my wallet and instead feel a sharp stab into my finger.

"Ouch, what the heck," I yelp.

"What happened?" Flynn asks.

"I don't know, my purse stabbed me."

I open my purse wide and look for my attacker. Carefully, I move around the objects on the bottom, still searching when my eye catches something red. I remove my wallet and find about a two-inch piece of Jack's red cup. I stare at it for a moment. I have to admit that I had actually put the shattered cup out of my mind and now here it is staring right at me pulling my thought back to it.

"What is it?" Abby asks, leaning over to get a look for herself.

"I guess Jack wanted to come with," I remark with a smile.

"Uh, I don't get it."

I reach back into my purse again and pull out the shard that had found its way into my purse when the cup shattered in front of us.

"Oh, honey. I am so sorry. Are you okay?" she asks me,

offering a hug.

"Actually, I'm good. It kind of feels like it was meant to be. A little piece of Jack is here with us and it feels right," I say with a smile.

I open my wallet, pull out my driver's license, put the piece of ceramic glass in the coin pocket, and zip it up.

After we return our paperwork and she takes a copy of our driver's license, we are directed to an upstairs office where we need to watch a short video.

Most of the information was the same as the waivers. "This is an extreme sport that can cause death." "If you die, it is not our fault and you cannot sue us." The part I found comical was the disclaimer about getting into our harnesses. "While your instructor is getting you harnessed up, there might be touching that under other circumstances could be considered inappropriate. Please know our instructors are professional and that any touching he or she does on your person is for your safety." Abby and I had to laugh like two twelve year old girls when we heard that.

Abby had a few moments of second thought when she got to the part about, "Should your instructor experience an issue such as a heart attack or stroke that causes them to lose consciousness the chute will automatically deploy at twenty-five hundred feet. At that time, you should reach for the straps that will fall down and do your best to steer back to the landing zone where our teams on the ground will be ready to assist you." I talked her off the ledge, and we all verbally confirmed we understood the information in the video and were instructed to *hang out* until we were called to the deck.

"Piper, Abby, and Flynn, you're on deck so let's get you suited up," the woman behind the window yells then directs us to stand in the large yellow squares on the floor where an instructor will meet us to put our harness on.

I start to blush when the hot Aussie catches my eye and is walking toward me. Abby gives me a nudge and a smile then mouths the words *Oh my gawd he is hot*. I nod in agreement while Flynn chuckles at our schoolgirl behavior.

"Hello again, you must be Piper. I'm Brandon. I will be your instructor today."

"Hello, yes I am," I say, extending my hand to shake his hand.

"Nah, that's way too formal for us, give me a high-five," he says, raising his hand in the air.

His accent is intoxicating, his excitement is contagious. You can tell that jumping out of planes is something he loves to do to the extreme and that he can't wait to get back up in the air.

I give him his high-five along with a nervous laugh. Two more instructors have joined us. Another Aussie named Gus and a good ole American boy named Todd. All good looking and fit guys, but Brandon is by far the hottest of them.

I'm too busy watching everyone around me to realize that Brandon is trying to talk to me.

"Oh, I'm sorry. I started daydreaming I guess."

"Ah, no worries. Let's get this harness on you," he replies with a smile.

"Gawd that smile is amazing." I didn't realize I was talking out loud until Abby and Flynn both dropped their jaws to the floor and Brandon blushed a little.

Pardon me while I go crawl into a hole and die now.

After getting our harness on and set, we all take a group picture and then we are being instructed to go wait in the "yard." They also told us to watch the sky for the divers that are getting ready to jump.

A moment later, we are watching the plane fly overhead and one by one, we see three black little dots falling from the plane. If you were standing anywhere else and saw this you would be in a panic, but here it is normal, here it is sane, here it makes sense and here we pay to jump out of a plane.

Less than a minute later, we see the chutes open and the three are safely floating to the ground. What I didn't expect was to be able to hear the sound of the chute opening while standing on the ground. The rippling sound of the fabric being let loose from the pack and the air grabbing a hold was mesmerizing. About Five minutes later the jumpers are on the ground safe and a minute after that the plane is landing. I found it hysterical that the jumpers made it back before the plane did. I will blame my outburst of laughter on my nerves.

"All right, Next team lets go," the pilot calls.

"Okay, Piper, here we go. Can you look into this camera for me?"

I look into a small camera he has mounted to his hand, he presses a button and asks me a few basic questions.

"Here we are on the glorious day. Piper, can you tell me how you are feeling?"

"Um, like I'm going crazy."

"Are you ready for this?"

"I guess we will find out."

"Okay good. All right, let's get you on the plane."

The plane ride up was shorter than I imagined. The instructors are busy making final adjustments to our harnesses and making sure we are attached to them securely. It hadn't dawned on me that I will be the first jumper since I was the last one to get on the plane, that is until Brandon gives me some final instructions that there is no way I am going to remember once I leave the safety of the plane. Then he waddles us to the door.

Looking out the open door was a bit of a shock, the wind coming in, the ground moving slowly below, the few clouds seem to be right at my feet. I place my feet on the tiny step that is right outside the door of the plane. Once I am stable I cross my arms over my chest and...wait...Oh my fucking hell. Is this truly about to happen... it's not too late... I can sti… woooooooaaaaah…

"AAAAAAAAAHHHHHHHHH."

"AAAHHHH."

"AAAAAAHHHHHH."

Before I knew it, Brandon was flipping us out of the plane into summersault. He stops the spin and we are flying with our hands out to our sides. He grabs my right arm and pulls it closer to our sides and we spin to the right. A moment later, he does the same thing with my left arm and we spin to the left. I can't help but smile. I can feel my skin flapping in the wind. It's strange, it doesn't feel like we are falling, and from what I heard in the hangar we are falling at about a hundred and forty miles per hour.

Brandon taps me on my shoulder letting me know he is about to deploy the chute. A second later, the chute opens and our fast fall is slowed to what feels like a float. I expected the sound of the chute to be much louder than it was.

Brandon makes some small adjustments to the harness and then reaches his hand in front of me to position the camera.

"So how you doing, how do you feel?"

"Wow, this is amazing. I understand the attraction to wanting to do this again and again."

"So you like it?"

"Like it? No, I love it. You feel so free up here."

Brandon turns the camera off and then grabs the ropes to steer us toward our landing zone. The ground is slowly getting closer, and when Brandon spots a cloud off to our right, he moves us closer and swings us into the foggy air. The ground disappears for a few movements. I move my arms out around me as if to try to grab a hold of the puffy cloud, of course, I only feel damp air. He swings us back out of the cloud, revealing the ground below us once more.

Before maneuvering us, he moves us into position to land. He asks how my stomach is doing.

"It's great, never better," I respond.

"Then get ready for some fun."

Before I have a chance to comprehend what is about to happen, he pulls down on the left steer cord. The chute veers us to the left, sending us spinning. Brandon then repeats the same to the right. I can see why he asked how my stomach was. I giggle and scream as he continues to switch from left to right until he pulls down on both, he put on the breaks as he called it.

"Okay, when I say when you need to push your legs out in front of you for landing."

"I can do that."

The ground seems as if it is moving faster as we get closer and before I know it, we are sliding in for our ground landing. With our feet or should I say butts safely on the ground, he unhooks the harness to detach me from him and then turns his attention to the falling parachute. It falls on top of us and he quickly moves to uncover us.

The group of jumpers waiting their turn let off a loud cheer as they watch me. Funny how the roles have reversed so quickly. My sky

diving adventure is ending. However, theirs is just beginning. A few moments later, Flynn and then Abby have landed and we are laughing with excitement.

"Holy shit, did we really just fucking do that?" Abby yells.

"I think we did, but it all happened so fast that I'm not actually sure."

"And that is why Jack wanted you to get a video, he wanted you to be able to look back on this over and over again," Flynn adds.

"Oh wow I actually forgot about the video," I say.

We walk back into the hangar where we get our harnesses removed and are directed to a small desk that I had not noticed before to pick up my video.

As I approach the desk, I can't stop thinking about how I

wish Jack had been here. He would have truly loved this. Then I remember the small piece of glass in my purse. As we wait for my video to be completed, I take a walk outside. Abby and Flynn start to follow but keep their distance.

I look around the grounds and see a small tree standing next to the gray building, and begin to walk toward it. Without thinking, I kneel down next to the tree and scrape away some of the dirt to make a small hole. I then retrieve the small piece of glass from my coin purse attached to my wallet and place it in the hole. Covering the hole with the loose dirt, I whisper, "You will always be a part of me, and I a part of you. I leave a piece of us here to mark the adventure we should have been able to take together."

Rae Matthews

Chapter Ten

Memories

After our awesome skydiving adventure, Abby and Flynn drop me off at home. They both offered to come in, but I think it is time for me to have some alone time. I know what is waiting for me when I get in there and I don't want them hanging around wanting to talk about it.

I cross my entryway and toss my purse onto the coffee table. It's strange how fast you get used to an empty house. The noises it makes that you never paid any attention to before, the way the floor squeaks when you step on the boards that have come slightly loose. I never used to pay attention to things like that, not like I didn't know the sounds, but when you are home alone, knowing that no one else will be joining you, the sounds are much different than they used to be.

As I round the corner into the kitchen, I see the pieces of the red coffee mug still lying scattered on the floor. I kneel down and start picking up the larger pieces and place them on the counter. The smaller ones I sweep up with the broom and dispose of them in the garbage.

After putting the broom back, I walk over to the counter where I had laid the rest. Standing over them, I contemplate what I should do with them. Should I throw them away? Should I try to glue them back together, or should I put them in a baggy and put them in a drawer?

"This is silly," I say to myself. "I have lost my damn mind," I add.

I slide the pieces into my hand and while shaking my head at my craziness, I walk over to the garbage to toss them in. As I open the lid to the garbage, I'm frozen. I cannot bring myself to do the sane thing and throw them away.

"Why is this so damn hard? It was a freaking cup?"

Before my mind can talk my body out of it, I place the broken pieces back on the counter. Run to the living room, grab my purse, and grab my keys. I am in my car pulling out of my driveway before I know it. I know I should not be doing this, I know I said the last time would be the last time. I'm not sure why there was a first time. It is actually kind of sick and twisted. Why would anyone do this to themselves? It can't help. It can only make things worse for me. Yet I find myself doing this at least once a week. I need to stop, I have to stop, it is not healthy.

Although I tried to talk myself out of it, I still find myself pulling into the large parking lot I have come to know. Without thinking, I turn off the car and start heading for the door. I nod to the woman leaving as I hold the door for her. The same ugly gray and blue carpet greets me as I walk toward the elevator.

I know I should turn around and leave, this is not right. If I can't tell Abby or Casey what I have been doing then, I shouldn't be doing it. I no more think Casey's name and I hear her voice.

"Piper!"

I turn to see Casey is walking toward me. Shit, what do I tell her, how can I explain why I am here... why is she here?

"Hey, what are you doing here?" I ask in the peppiest

voice I can muster.

"Some jerk tripped at a house I was showing him and his wife was threatening to sue the sellers, so I brought him in for an x-ray to prove there was nothing wrong with him other than a scraped palm. Asshole," she explains.

"Wow, some people are out for only themselves."

"I know it is freaking sad. So what are you doing here...wait. How was today?" she asks with excitement.

Here is my chance, my chance to distract her with the details of my recent skydive. I quickly start talking and slowly start walking us to the door. She is so mesmerized by the story she has all but forgotten I didn't tell her why I was at the hospital.

In what seems like forever, I have spilled every last drop of detail I can think in time for us to approach my car. I have my keys in hand ready to make my escape.

"It was so amazing. I wish you could have been there with us, you would have loved it."

"Oh hell no, you are not getting me to jump out of a plane unless it is on fire and I have no other choice." She laughs.

I smile and use my key fob to unlock my door in the hopes she will let me leave without coming back around to why I am here.

"I'm gonna get going. I'm getting hungry and dinner won't cook itself." I joke.

"Sure thing and I have to stop at the office to fill out some paperwork on this asshole. Call me later if you want to chat some more," she adds and walks away.

Thank God. I can't believe that worked. I can't believe I almost got caught. All the more reason why I should stop doing this to myself. Casey would have ripped me a new one if she had found out. Abby would have lectured me on how damaging it is. Then there is Flynn, he might actually understand. Granted he would think I was still a little batshit crazy for doing it, but he would understand my need.

Pulling back into my driveway, I am relieved that I am

finally home. I'm still no closer to my answers about the cup, but I'm not exposed either.

Walking back into my kitchen, I open the fridge to weigh my options for dinner. I haven't been grocery shopping yet so my options are a little limited. My eyes glance at the pieces on the counter again. I let out a loud "UUUUHHHH" and slam the refrigerator door. I grab my phone and pull up my contacts.

"Thank you for calling Pizza Hut, this is Adam. What can we make fresh for you today?"

"Hey, Adam, it's Piper. Can I get my usual?"

"Oh for sure, anything for you, doll. It will be about thirty minutes."

"Thanks, Adam."

I hang up and toss my phone gently onto the center island. While I wait for my dinner, I decide it is a good time for wine. Wine makes everything clearer, that is until the next morning, and you realize one bottle turned into three and your head is yelling at you. Luckily, Abby is not here or it would turn into one of those nights.

I pour myself a glass of Moscato then retrieve my small velvet box from the hutch. Taking a seat at the dining room table, I slowly open the box, take a sip of wine, then retrieve the folded paper from inside. Scanning the list carefully, I find what I am looking for and cross it off.

~~Skydive~~

Scanning the list again, I pay closer attention to the ones that were already crossed off.

~~Fall in love~~
~~Do a polar plunge~~
~~Win a contest~~

Volunteer my time
Take a walk with my mom
Go fishing with my dad

I remember each of them as if they were yesterday. The polar plunge Jack, Flynn, and I did barely a week after I made the list. Being the first week of March in the Midwest, we froze our respective asses off. I immediately regretted showing Jack my list at that point. He saw polar plunge and immediately signed us up for the senior plunge. I swear, whoever thought jumping into a lake in freezing temperatures was absolutely, positively insane, and the fact that we have kept this tradition for so many years makes the rest of us positively as insane as they were.

The funny part was that to make it fun and goofy we dressed up as Alvin and the chipmunks. Okay, it wasn't originally our idea to dress up—it was also part of the tradition to dress up or something equally as funny. Most guys came in some form of drag and most girls wore anything that let them have on as much clothing as possible. After we made our jump, we swore we would never in a million years, even if our lives depended on it, would we ever and I mean ever do it again. To this day, we never have.

Again, why is this still a tradition? Has no one come up with a better idea, or do we think that this is a good idea. Okay, so it did seem like a good idea at the time. However, afterward it seemed like it took us a month to thaw out, plus I ended up getting the flu and missing a few days of school. Half the senior class and me.

I did win a contest ironically. Even though it was pretty silly, I still count it as a win. That May, the local radio station was giving tickets for a special viewing of Jurassic Park in June. It was a VIP pass that included four tickets, free popcorn, pop, a candy choice, and a tee shirt.

All you had to do was call in and answer three questions.

I ran to my phone and dialed the station's number repeatedly until I got ringing instead of a busy signal.

"Hi, you're caller number ten. What's your name," the DJ said when he answered the line.

"Oh my God, really?" I scream into the phone.

"Yes, you are. What's your name, hon."

"Piper, my name is Piper. This is so cool."

"All right, Piper, here is your first question. True or false, the name dinosaur means 'terrible lizard'?"

"Oh man, um, geez, I will go with true."

"DING DING DING, you are cooooorrect."

"I had no idea. That was totally a guess."

"It was a good guess. Okay, for your second question, a person who studies fossils and prehistoric life such as dinosaurs is known as a what?"

"Oh, oh I know this one. It is a paleontologist."

"DING DING DING, you are coooooorrect again. One more and you win the prize pack. All right for your third and final question, which came first, the Jurassic or Triassic period?"

"Oh, I think this is a trick question. You totally want me to say Jurassic since that is the movie so I'm going with Triassic period."

"DING DING DING, you got it!! You are our winner!"

Winning that contest was the best. Jack, Flynn, Casey, and I all got to see the best movie of the summer. Actually, it was the first and last movie we saw that summer. After the pregnancy test came up positive, we didn't do a whole lot that cost money.

Most of the summer was spent doing the little things that would become harder to do after the baby came. Therefore, taking a walk with my mom and going fishing with my dad were easy things to cross off. Then there was the day that Jack said he loved me. Yes, we thought we were in love with each other long before, but we had agreed not to be one of those high school couples who went around kissing and declaring their love and then a week later they had broken up and were off declaring their love to someone new.

No, we were not going to be that kind of couple. We agreed that we would not say those words until we knew we were actually going to mean it.

I remember it was October and I was about five months pregnant. We went for a walk to look at the leaves changing color before they fall to the ground and the snow comes. We stopped at a large oak tree and Jack pulled out a disposable camera from his jacket pocket.

"Stop right there," he said.

"Jack, stop I look like a house," I joked.

"No you don't. You look amazing, and I want to remember this day for the rest of my life," he told me.

I leaned against the tree, held my belly, looked at the camera, and smiled. He snapped a picture and wound the film as a jogger was passing by.

"Excuse me, could you please take our picture?" he asked the man.

The man agreed and Jack ran to me, knelt down, kissed my belly, and pulled a small box from his other pocket.

"I may not be the man you dreamed of, but you are the woman of my dreams. This may not be the life you expected to live, but I am glad I am in it. I know we are young and I know we are scared of what comes next, but today I make you this promise. Through the good times and bad, I will love you forever. I promise to do my best to make you the happiest woman in the world if you will make me the happiest man and say yes."

The world seemed to disappear. The jogger that was once standing in front of us was a blur. Jack opened the small box and in it was a ring. It was small but breathtaking, in my eyes.

In that moment, I knew that I was truly in love with him and that I would always be in love with him.

"YES, YES, YES!" I screamed and knelt down to kiss

him over and over.

We start laughing and giggling as we fell to the ground and I kept kissing him. The jogger kept snapping pictures until there was one picture left. Jack and I finally stood up and posed next to the tree for the final picture.

That night I got home and crossed fall in love off my list, folded it back up, and put in back in its drawer. That was the last time I saw the list. The last four months of my pregnancy flew by and the next thing I knew I had little baby Bryna to look after.

The doorbell interrupts my stroll down memory lane. After paying the delivery guy, I bring dinner back to the table and once again look at my list. I see many things on the list that I have actually already done over the years. I decide I should update my list and see how much is actually left. The first is take a picture in the same spot for each season. I did that with Bryna the year she turned five. But as I start to cross it off my list, I realize that Jack left them untouched for a reason. I know he knows some of these were done, I mean hello, marry my best friend is right there below fall in love, which is crossed off.

"Hmm, maybe I should wait until Jack's little adventure is done," I say to myself.

"It's not like the list is going anywhere," I continue.

I fold the list back up and place the pen and paper back in the velvet box. I go into the kitchen and grab a sandwich bag and the broken pieces of Jack's mug to put them carefully into the baggie and zip it closed.

"I will see you next month," I say as I place the box and the baggie back on the hutch.

Chapter Eleven

Annie Oakley

Now that I am finally back to volunteering at the shelter, my days have flown by faster and faster. They offered me a paid position, but with the life insurance sitting in the bank and the shelter struggling to raise money all the time, I declined their offer to pay me. I would still do the extra work and instead I wrote them a check for more money than they have ever seen. Why I waited so long to make a donation was beyond me. However, it is better late than never.

I'm finishing my shift when I get a text.

FLYNN: What time will you get off work?
ME: I will be done in about twenty minutes, why?
FLYNN: Are you coming right home?
ME: Not like I have a hugely active social life.
FLYNN: So that is a yes then
ME: That would be a yes, are you going to tell me why?
FLYNN: You will see.
ME: Jack?

FLYNN: Guess you will find out…
ME: Jerk
FLYNN: Thank you
ME: that wasn't a compliment
FLYNN: I think it was

I laugh at our banter and get excited to finish cleaning the rest of the cat litter boxes so I can get home and find out what is next on Jack's list. It has to be a Carpe Diem adventure otherwise why else would Flynn need to know what time I would be home.

Granted, he has been at the house a lot lately. It seems like when it rains, it pours. After fixing my dryer he had to come over and fix a small leak in the bathroom faucet, the ceiling fan in the bedroom, and the garbage disposal took a crap last week.

I'm lucky to have him around and for him to be so handy with tools. Jack truthfully knew how to pick a best friend. Flynn could not have been a better friend to Jack, and now to me.

Twenty-five short minutes later, I pull up to my house and see Flynn's car. I was kind of expecting to see everyone here, but it looks as if it is only Flynn. I park my car in the driveway and announce, "I'm home" as I walk through the door.

I don't see Flynn anywhere and he is not answering me.

"Heeeelllooo, anyone there?" I call out.

Nothing, not a word. Okay, so I guess this is a game of hide and go seek? I toss my purse on the couch and make my way to the kitchen, but stop when I see an envelope on the dining room table.

I was right! With childlike excitement, I race to the table and rip it open to learn the details of what Jack had planned next.

Piper,

Here we are again, another month has gone by and another adventure awaits you. I will take it easy on you this month and will teach you a new skill.

I have to admit I was a little surprised you added this to your list, but I agree every woman should know how to shoot a gun. And not those kinds of guns you see in the video games at the mall.

I reserved a spot just for us at the range, so you don't have to worry about shooting anyone. Just kidding, well not really.

Jack

His words bring a smile to my face. Jack was always a bit of a joker. Just as I am folding the letter, Flynn comes around the corner from the kitchen with a big smile on his face.

"So I guess it's you and me on this one," Flynn announces.

"I guess so. Did you bring your body armor?" I laugh.

"Nope, only the guns. Did you want to change or anything before we go?" he asks.

"Yes, I *really* need to get out of these clothes, maybe take a quick shower... Do I have time?" I ask.

"Sure, about fifteen minutes."

"You did not actually reserve the whole range did you? You didn't know what time I was getting off work?"

"Jack had planned to reserve it for the whole day today. He wasn't sure what time he was going to take you so he wanted the whole day to make it look spontaneous."

"I see. He really did have all this planned out didn't he? Wait then why do I only have fifteen minutes?"

"Yep, like I said, he put years into planning this, and the place does close at some point. I want to get there with plenty of time for you to be able to shoot as much as you want. Now go get ready."

"All the guns? How many did you bring?"

"Go get ready, you will see when we get there. Now go before I pick you up and throw you in the shower with all your clothes on," Flynn replies, amused.

I give him a squinty-eyed smile and dash up the stairs to get ready. I'm not sure how, but I managed to shower, get dressed and even put on some makeup with about two minutes to spare.

"Okay I'm ready, oh wait. I almost forgot."

Flynn gives me an odd look as he watches me walk over to the hutch and retrieve a piece of the mug. I put it in my back pocket and put the bag back on the shelf next to the velvet box.

"Don't give me that look," I say jokingly.

"Hey, whatever you gotta do." He smiles.

"I know I'm weird. There is something wrong with me isn't there?" I ask.

"Nah, we all grieve in our own ways. If you want to carry around a broken piece of glass in honor of your dead husband, then you go right ahead and do that."

"Well, when you say it like that it sounds like you should be taking me to the nut farm and not a shooting range," I say, punching him in the arm.

"How do you know that is not the plan?" He laughs back.

"Whatever, let's go."

A short drive out of town later, we pull up to a large white building with only one other car in the parking lot. I actually feel bad that Jack reserved the whole day. I'm sure the worker has been bored off his or her ass today.

Walking into the building, I'm a little nervous, looking at the large cases Flynn is carrying. I've never shot a gun before. I've never even held a gun before. I'm not entirely sure why I thought to put it on my list.

After walking through the front door, you are stopped by a locked second door. To the right there is a small sliding window. We wait only a moment before a man comes to the window to greet us.

"I'm sorry we are closed for an event today," he tells us.

"Yes, I'm Flynn Avery and this is Piper Reynolds."

"Oh, hello, sir. Come right in I have been expecting you, I will meet you on the other side."

The door buzzes and we are able to walk through to the large building. It is not anything like I expected, not that I had an idea what to expect. The man that greeted us exits a door to meet us.

"Mr. Avery, did you decide on the indoor or outdoor range?" he asks.

"Well, it's a little chilly out so let's start inside so she can concentrate."

"Sounds good, please follow me."

He leads us to a red door. When he opens it, he escorts us into a room with five lanes with cement dividers separating each lane.

"You have your choice of lanes. Each lane has been set up for you with a target and the extras are hanging on the wall of each lane. Let me know if you need anything, I will be up front," he tells us and then excuses himself.

I am in awe of this place. The idea of coming here only to shoot targets is a little beyond me. I guess I am about to find out what all the fuss is about.

Flynn opens the smaller of the cases revealing the two handguns he has in it. One looks like it would fit in my hand nicely and the other looks like a hand cannon. The thing is huge! Who would want that and why in the heck would they even need it, I wonder.

"Okay, you ready for this?" Flynn asks.

"We are here so I should probably shoot them at least once I suppose."

"All right then. We are going to start you off with the smaller one. It is a 9mm Ruger. Now it does have some kick, just to warn you."

He takes his time showing me all the parts of the gun. He has me hold the gun unloaded so I can get used the feel of it. He teaches me about the gun's safety, how when the little button is red the safety is off. To help me remember he tells me.

"Always remember RID. Red Is Dead."

I nod.

"Remember, never point a gun at anything you are not willing to shoot or kill."

I nod again.

"Also, always know your target and beyond."

"What does that mean?" I ask.

"I mean that when you shoot a gun, make sure that if you miss you are not going to hurt something or someone else."

A few more tips and, supposedly, I was ready to shoot. Flynn and I walk over to lane number one. He puts the empty gun and the clip on the ledge in front of me. He instructs me to put my earmuffs and safety glasses on.

"Now go ahead and pick up the gun, take your stance, don't forget to put one in the chamber," he tells me.

I do as he says then look to him for more instruction. He moves in close and helps place my arms and legs in the correct shooting stance. I realize this is the first time anyone has been this close to me since Jack died. It feels a little strange. I have known Flynn forever, and he must have touched me, or been close to me a thousand times. Why does this feel any different? Flynn brings my attention back to the gun when he tells me to breathe normally and when I exhale, pause for a second, and then pull the trigger.

As I slowly pull the gun up and aim at the center of the target, I feel Flynn wrap his arms around me to hold up my arms with me.

"Okay, so just breathe normally, inhale, exhale, trigger."

BANG!!

My arms fly up from the kick of the gun. It is insane on how loud the firing was even with my earmuffs tightly hugging my ears. I look over my shoulder to Flynn.

"Do I shoot it again?" I ask with a smile.

"Whenever you are ready, go ahead."

I look back to the target and again aim the gun down range and prepare the fire. Flynn is against my back helping to hold my arms in position.

BANG!! BANG!! BANG!!

I fire off three rounds back to back and then place the gun on the shelf in front of me. Removing my earmuffs, I turn to look at Flynn.

"That is actually kind of fun. I'm not sure I would make a hobby out of it, but I can see where that would blow off some aggression."

Flynn laughs and then pushes a small button on the wall beside us. The target starts to move closer, and closer until it is right in front of us.

"Hmm, I didn't do so great did I," I say, looking at my holes that were far outside the center ring of the target.

"Honestly, you did better than I thought you would. You at least hit the target all four times. With some practice, you would be a great shot."

"So should I keep shooting this gun?"

"It's your adventure, you can do what you want to do."

We continue to practice with the 9mm for another half hour before Flynn checks the barrel and it was getting too hot to continue using it. I have to admit that I was a little disappointed, but I had shot almost a hundred rounds into all the targets that were prehung for us.

I had shot several rounds and then moved on to the next lane. By the time we got to the end, most of my holes were in the smaller circles, not dead center, but the two black ones around that. I did manage to get one in the little red circle and started jumping for joy until Flynn took the gun away from me, reminding me I still had two rounds in it.

Flynn replaced all the targets and brought out the cannon. This thing was massive. The idea that people own these things were pretty scary. Flynn tells me it is a Smith and Wesson model 500. The barrel must be at least eight inches long. He explains to me the basic differences between the 9mm that I just shot and this. The 9mm has a clip with seven shots; this is a revolver style and has six. The other one would fire each time I pulled the trigger where this one I have to pull the hammer back each time to fire.

When Flynn hands me the cannon, unloaded, I nearly drop it to the ground. I expected it to be heavy, though not that heavy. I actually need both hands to hold it.

"Wow, I'm not sure I will be able to aim this one very well."

"Piper, if you actually manage to pull it up and fire it, I will be impressed. With this one there is no way you are going to hit the target." He laughs.

I accept his challenge and offer a wager of sorts.

"So are you willing to put your money where your mouth is?" I ask.

"Well, I suppose if you are willing to lose it I am willing to take it."

"If I hit the target, you buy dinner tonight. If I don't hit it, I will buy dinner, deal?"

"It's your money."

Flynn takes back the gun and puts one bullet in it. He spins the cylinder and pops it closed. He sets the gun on the shelf in front of the lane and places his earmuffs on.

"Whenever you are ready?"

I smile, nod, and turn to face the lane as I put my earmuffs and safety glasses back on. When ready, I pull up the gun and line up the site with the red dot on the target. I remind myself to breathe, inhale, exhale, inhale, exhale. Man, this gun is heavy; my arms are starting to shake. Inhale, exhale… BANG!

My arms fly above my head, my hands fighting to keep a hold of the large gun. Now I know why he only put one bullet in. My arms come back down as gravity demands, and

I can feel my jaw on the floor.

"You could have warned me about that kick."

"What fun would that have been?" Flynn says laughing and reaching for the gun.

I look down the lane at the target to see if I came close to hitting it. I don't see anything so I start to squint. Flynn pushes the button to bring it in for a closer look.

"So when you said I wouldn't hit the target…"

"Yeah."

"What did that mean?"

"That I was right in thinking that you wouldn't hit the paper at all. Looks like I win."

"So this little half hole, partial tear sort of thing on the right side here… that should count since it did, in fact, hit the paper, right?" I ask with a smirk.

Flynn's happy little I win smile falls as he inspects the tear. He even goes so far as the reach out with his right hand to feel for texture difference.

"I guess technically that was probably made by your bullet."

"So that would mean that I am actually the winner here," I tell him, adding in my own little happy dance.

Flynn rolls his eyes and starts to pack up the guns. I think I have had about enough of the cannon.

"Okay, you ready for some rifle action?"

"You know, I think I'm good with the guns. Maybe some other time you can bring me back and we can shoot the rifles. I am actually getting hungry."

"Okay, just one last thing before we leave."

Flynn pulls a camera out of one of the cases and hands me the 9mm and one of my targets. He has me pose in front of one of the lanes and snaps a picture.

While Flynn packs up his guns and talks to the attendant, I take the opportunity to take care of something myself.

I exit the large building and look around. Not a ton of options here, I think to myself. It is mainly grass and parking lot out front. I walk around the side of the building where I saw the outdoor range in the back.

Pulling out the glass from my back pocket, I scan the area for its perfect home. I need a spot that no one will find it accidentally and throw it away. With not many options available close by, I finally decide to walk the long distance to the end of the outdoor range where there is a large hill and a long tree line that wraps around the outdoor shooting lanes.

The air is a little chilly as the weather is starting to change. I love this time of year, the crisp air smell, the look of the trees as they start to turn their fall colors. It does not take me long to get to the tree line and find the perfect spot. An odd-looking tree that looks like it was split in half and rather than die, each side grew strong and tall. I find a spot in the middle of the trunk and dig a small hole. I place the red glass in the hole and cover it.

As I pack the dirt down, I feel Flynn behind me. Watching me, wanting nothing more than to talk, but respecting my need for silence.

As I stand up, I brush off the dirt and grass from the knees of my jeans. Flynn walks closer and puts his hand on my shoulder.

"You okay?" he asks softly.

"I think so. I… Um…" I fumble as I attempt to explain my madness.

"You don't have to say anything, I get it."

"It is weird though, right?"

"Everyone grieves in their own way. Nothing about what you are doing is strange."

I offer a smile and before walking with Flynn back to the car, I kiss my hand, kneel down, and lay it on the ground over the buried piece.

"I love you."

Chapter Twelve

Pay up

The hostess shows us to our seat, lets us know the specials and that our waitress will be right with us, and then leaves us.

"So shall I get the steak or the lobster, or better yet, the steak *and* the lobster?" I joke.

"Laugh it up, chuckles."

"Oh poor baby, is someone a cranky loser today?"

"Not a bit. Order whatever you like, but I wouldn't brag too loud, you didn't win by much and remember payback is a dish best served cold."

"That's revenge. Payback is a bitch," I correct him.

"Whatever, you know what I mean," he says, then buries his face into the menu.

The waitress soon comes to greet us and takes our order. I decided to go with the prime rib, no lobster, and Flynn orders the crab legs. The Maple is one of the nicer restaurants in the area. They are well known for their crab legs, but I had a huge craving for a good steak.

Jack was the master griller in our house and for some

reason, I have not been able to make a decent steak since he has been gone.

Flynn and I haven't stopped talking since we got here. Even when the food arrives, we stop only long enough for our waitress to place our plates in front of us and thank her. Once our conversation turns to memories of Jack, we take turns telling each other our favorite memories. Our laughter at some of our trip down memory lane landed us a stern warning to please keep it down. Jack never let life bring him down. Even during some of the most difficult times, he would always find a way to make someone laugh.

"Oh yeah, Jack *really* knew how to make a fool of himself," I say, as Flynn finishes one of his stories.

"He sure did," Flynn responds.

"Flynn can I ask you a question?"

"Sure."

"Why did you stay?" I ask.

"What do you mean?"

"When I found out I was pregnant, why did you stay here instead of going off to college?"

Flynn puts his fork down and leans back in his chair.

"That is kind of a hard question to answer. I think it was because I had seen my life in a certain way and going away to college wasn't what I saw for myself. The only reason I was going to go was because Jack was going. I thought it would be fun. When his plans changed, I had no reason to go."

"So has your vision of life worked out?"

"For the most part. I knew I wanted to stay in town, I never saw myself living anywhere else."

"So why didn't you ever get married?"

"Hmm, well I guess I would have to say never found the right girl."

"The *right* girl? Flynn, you have dated some awesome women. How could none of them have been right for you?"

"I'm not sure what to tell ya. None of them ever

measured up to what I was looking for. I guess maybe I'm simply meant to be a bachelor for life." He laughs.

It always amazed me that Flynn never got married. When Bryna was younger, he was so good with her. He would lie on the floor and play Barbie's with her. As she got a little older, he allowed her to dress him up for the tea party. I used to think that one day he was going to make a great dad.

I'm not sure what made me ask my next question, the wine, the thought that he is not married or rarely dating anyone, or the fact that he stayed in town with Jack. Oh Jack. The common theme, looking back on everything, was Jack. Was he in love with Jack?

"Flynn, are you gay?"

"What makes you think I'm gay?" he says, exploding into laughter.

I feel my face turn a bright red with embarrassment. What was I thinking? I should have known better then to think he was gay. I couldn't help myself. He *was* showing some signals so it wasn't a totally unwarranted question.

"Let me see, there is the fact that you're not married, you don't date much, you were always attached to Jack's hip... I guess I thought maybe there was a chance..." I stop myself before I finish that sentence.

"What, a chance that I was in love with Jack?" he asks very seriously.

"I guess I thought there was a chance yes."

"No, Piper, I am not gay and I was not in love with Jack. If I were, I would have told him and you."

"I just thought... well we all have our secrets."

"I may have many secrets, Piper, but being gay is not one of them."

I look deep into his eyes. Many secrets? I give him a squinty-eye look and add in a smile as if to let him know I am interested in hearing about his *many* secrets. Flynn smiles back and shakes his head.

"Oh no, this is not the time or place for me to be airing

out any skeletons." He laughs.

"Come on. If you don't tell me, I will have to assume I was right and that you are gay." I laugh.

"Piper, you *really* don't want to know my secrets. Jack knew them and that was bad enough."

The mood gets a little awkward after that. When the waitress finally brings the bill, I am relieved. Flynn seems a little put off by my line of questioning. I never took him for someone easily offended or maybe I hit a nerve. He may not be gay, but there is definitely something bothering him.

Jack knew and never told me so it can't be that bad. I decide not to press the subject. If he wants to tell me what was on his mind, he will, in his own time.

When Flynn drops me off at my house, I offer him a nightcap, but he declines.

"I'm truthfully sorry if I offended you or pressed you too hard on anything tonight," I offer as an attempt to restore the mood,

"Piper, you didn't offend me. You could never offend me."

"Are you sure? You're okay?"

"I'm fine, I had a lot of fun tonight. I'm ready to get home, unbutton my pants, and relax, I think I ate way too much," he says with a smile.

"Okay, as long as we are okay," I respond.

"Yes, everything is fine. I will talk to you tomorrow."

I exit the car and Flynn waits for me to get in the house and turn the lights on before he waves then drives away. Still feeling weird about how things were left, I decide to give Abby a call to see what she thinks.

"You asked him what?" Abby yells into the phone.

"I know, but that would certainly answer a lot of questions if he was," I point out.

"Yes that would indeed answer a ton of questions, but I don't see him being gay. Like at all."

"Me either, but you never know. My thought was that if he was and never knew how to tell us that if I brought it up that it might be easier for him to come out. But then he said Jack knew his secrets."

"I don't think he is mad, and of course, Jack knew his secrets. I know all yours and I don't tell anyone, especially Dave."

"So you think he is fine? It ended so weirdly," I ask as I remember those words, *you don't know all my secrets.*

"I do. I mean he is a guy, he probably needed to get home to take a shit after eating all that food."

I laugh at Abby's explanation and decide that on some level she is probably right. Flynn and I have known each other for years. If he was going to get mad at me because of a question, then he should hate me for some of the things in our past.

Like the time he asked me to cut his hair and I forgot to put a guard on the clippers and accidently shaved his head. Or the time that he asked me if I wanted to clean his house for some extra cash. Things were going great until I decided to do his laundry and accidently shrunk his favorite shirt. Oops.

After thinking about all the things he should have been pissed off at me for and wasn't, I have to agree with Abby.

After hanging up, I pull down the velvet box and prepare to cross off yet another item. I scan my list, looking for my latest adventure and cross it off.

~~Learn how to shoot a gun~~

Chapter Thirteen
Everyone Loves Spam

Holidays, they say, are the hardest after the death of a loved one. If it were not for everyone offering to come to my house for Thanksgiving, I think I would have had a mental breakdown this year. Last year was hard not having Jack around, but it still felt so surreal. Those that say the first year is the hardest must have found some magic pill that takes the pain away, I feel like this year is even harder.

Bryna took the week off work and is spending her whole holiday break with me. I am so excited to have her home and look forward to spending some time together.

Flynn called a few days ago and let me know that for my November Carpe Diem item we will all be taking a cooking class on Wednesday.

I had to laugh because I'm not the horrible cook I used to be. The only reason I added that to my list was because at the time I couldn't even boil water. Jack and Bryna endured many years of burnt and sometimes unrecognizable food before I finally got the hang of things.

Bryna is still asleep in her room. I didn't want to wake

her just yet. She has been working so hard at school and we have been staying up late talking. Flynn won't be here for a few hours so she will still have time to get ready.

I follow my morning routine of drinking my coffee and doing some cleaning. I've even started my morning walks again, but I will not walk today. Today I will make a visit that I know I should not. I haven't been there in over a month, so I'm not sure why I feel the need to do it today. Maybe it is because tomorrow is Thanksgiving. It should be a day that I am thankful for what I have so why I feel the need to do this to myself. It just makes me mad and fills me with grief.

Although I tried to talk myself out of it, I once again find myself sitting in the hospital parking lot. I haven't yet gotten out of the car. Maybe just sitting here will satisfy my uncontrollable need.

"I will not go in, I will not go in, I will not go in," I tell myself.

A half hour later, I fail in my attempt to talk myself out of it and find myself shutting off my car and opening the door. I grab my purse and yet again find myself waiting for the all too familiar elevator. When the door opens, I see Nancy, the day nurse, behind the door.

"Oh, Piper. Not today," she blurts out.

"No? Why not?" I asked, confused.

"There are way too many people up there. Someone might recognize you," she tells me.

"Oh," I say as I hang my head.

"I'm sorry. Any other day you know I would help you, but I just can't today."

"I understand, I don't want you to get in trouble."

"Honey, I'm sorry."

I smile and turn to walk back to my car.

"I hope you have a happy holiday," Nancy calls to me.

I turn slightly and wave as I wish her a happy holiday in return.

Getting back into my car, I am slightly relieved that Nancy caught me when she did. Had I gone in there and someone recognized me, I would have had no excuse for my behavior. Then there is the part of me that is sad that I was not caught. Maybe if I had, I would be able to stop my visits, if nothing else out of pure shame.

When I return home, I find Bryna just waking up and pouring the last of the coffee into a mug. I wish her a good morning as I take off my coat. I had hoped she would still be sleeping when I got home.

"Where did you go?" she asks.

"Oh, just wanted to clear my head so I went for a drive," I lie.

After a brief conversation about how she slept, I excuse myself and run up to take a hot shower and start getting ready.

I start the shower and begin to undress. As I look at myself in the mirror, I can't stop thinking about Jack. How he would have had me committed if he knew what I was doing.

I am finally able to brush off my disappointment in myself and make myself what I know will be an empty promise to never go there again.

"Mom, Flynn will be here soon," Bryna yells up to me an hour later.

"I know. Honey. I will be down in a minute," I yell back as I finish putting my makeup on.

I know Bryna is excited. This will be the first time she has been on one of my Carpe Diem days since the first dinner.

Before I know it, Flynn is knocking at the door and Bryna is flying to answer it.

"Flynn!" she yells and gives him a big hug.

"Bryna!" he yells, equaling her enthusiasm.

I sit back and laugh as they kid around with each other.

"So you ready to learn how to cook? You must be getting sick of mac & cheese and ramen noodles by now," Flynn asks.

"Hey I can cook, just last night I made Mom and I dinner."

"So was it mac & cheese or ramen?"

"It was spaghetti, for your information." She laughs.

"Oh yeah, 'cause you need a degree from the school of culinary arts to make that," he jokes.

Bryna punches him in the arm and lets out a pretend to be insulted gasp. Gee, I wonder where she gets that from?

"You ladies ready?" Flynn asks, rubbing his arm.

"Yep, I just have to grab one more thing," I say.

Once again, I walk over to the hutch and grab a piece of the cup. I had not told Bryna about what I am doing with the shards yet. I thought I would let her in on my little quirk in person.

"What's that?" she asks.

"Remember how I told you Dad's mug broke?"

"Yes."

"Well it's a long story, but I have been leaving a piece of the mug at each of the things I have been doing."

"Huh?" she says, giving me a confused look.

"I will tell you all about it on the way." I laugh.

We pile into Flynn's car and I begin to explain how when the mug broke a piece must have flown into my purse and how it poked me when I reached for my wallet when we went skydiving. I continued telling her how it had made me feel better knowing even a piece of her dad had been with me that day.

Then I told her that while waiting for my video, I saw a tree and how I knelt down and buried it and that it gave me a little bit of peace so I decided to leave a piece of him where ever my adventure took me. By the end of the story, we were both in tears.

"That is possibly the most perfect thing you could have ever thought to do with Dad's mug."

"So you don't think it's weird or anything?" I ask, wiping the tears away.

"Mom. No. Dad would have liked that," she answers.

Flynn had been quiet through my story and only offered a smile and a comforting hand when I needed it to help me get the words out.

We pull into the parking lot just as Bryna and I finish wiping our tears. Flynn offers to drive around the block a few times if we need more time, which makes us both laugh. He finds a parking spot close to the door and before you know it, we are walking into Savory Cooking and Catering.

We are greeted by a man wearing a chef coat and hat. He is all smiles from ear to ear.

"Ah, Flynn, these must be the lovely ladies you told me so much about," he says, reaching over to give us a kiss on each cheek.

"These are none other," Flynn says with a smile, looking back at me.

"Oh, honey. You didn't tell me they were so gorgeous."

"What can I say, I guess I never noticed," Flynn jokes.

"Sugar, no false words have ever been spoken in my presence. You know, these dolls are breathtaking." Chef laughs waving his hand "Well anyway, sweetie, I am Chef Basil. You can call me Chef.

"Basil? Is that your real name?" I ask.

"Oh no honey, but Chef Burns just doesn't have a nice ring to it if you know what I mean."

"I agree. I am Piper and this is my daughter, Bryna," I say.

"The pleasure is all mine. Now let's get you in here and start cooking," Chef says as he waves us in.

Chef Basil sets us up at our own cooking station since we are the only ones here. I assume Jack wanted to have the class all to ourselves again. You know, in case I started a fire or something.

"Okay, so I have to tell you, when Mr. Flynn here told me the theme for today's menu I was a little shocked. I mean I have never been asked for anything like this before. But I think I have come up with some fun recipes for you all to cook up today," Chef tells us as he uncovers the center island holding our ingredients.

"SPAM? We are cooking with Spam," I shout with laughter.

"Yes, ma'am, you are. Mr. Flynn here told me this was all your Mr. Jack's idea and who am I to change the wishes of your dearly departed," Chef playfully sasses back.

"No, it's fine. It's just he didn't really like Spam, so it kind of surprised me that's all," I say, still laughing.

What on earth was Jack thinking? Granted I love Spam, he was the one that thought meat from a can was just weird and refused to eat it. I have gotten so used to not buying it that I actually had forgotten how much I liked it.

Before we begin prepping our work areas, Flynn walks over and hands me another letter. But before I open it, Flynn tells me that Jack hadn't finished his letter so Flynn wrote me this letter.

I look at him in shock. Was the last letter the last I would receive. My eyes start to gloss over, but before the tears fully have a chance to take over Flynn puts his hand on my shoulder.

"Oh no, I have a few more, but this one he hadn't really written. I suppose he wasn't as sure what he wanted to say about Spam," Flynn tells me, adding a smile.

"Yeah, I mean what is there to really say about Spam." I laugh, taking a deep breath and open the letter.

Piper & Bryna,

Spam, Spam, I love Spam... Said no one, ever. However, today we come here with open minds and empty bellies for the possibility of finding a new love of Spam. May the Pepto be with us, we are going to need it.

Flynn

P.S. Jack was hoping to use today's menu as inspiration for your Thanksgiving dinner, but if I could make one small request, can you please still make us a turkey. And I don't mean turkey-flavored Spam.

I have to laugh when I finish reading Flynn's letter and hand it over to Bryna to read. She starts laughing and gives Flynn a hug.

"Oh my gosh, that is the sweetest thing I have ever seen," Chef blurts. "Oh I'm sorry, I didn't mean to interrupt your little moment there," he adds as we all look over to him.

"You're fine. Should we get started?"

"Oh, honey. You took the words right out of my mouth."

Chef begins by passing around the recipe cards we will be using, and then instructs us to retrieve our ingredients from the center island.

We do as we are instructed and are soon creating what he calls our Spamtastic masterpieces. First we open our sealed cans of Spam and cut it into two-inch-by-two-inch cubes. Next we take our bacon and cut it in half and begin wrapping the cubes with the bacon then stick a toothpick in to hold the bacon in place. Next we set our ovens to 325 degrees and place our pan of bacon-covered Spam into the oven as it preheats. Chef tells us to make sure the oven is not preheated before you put the pan in or the bacon will cook too fast and burn before the Spam is fully heated.

Next we follow our instructions to make a puff pastry and he mentions that if we are in a hurry we can use the store bought, thawed puff pastry sheets you can get at the grocery store.

After mixing the apples, cranberries, and other ingredients needed for the turnover filling, we add in the Spam and begin putting our turnovers together.

By this time, the bacon is cooked so we remove them from the oven and bump the heat up to 350 for the Spam apple turnovers to cook. Chef offers us a break and a chance to try our bacon-covered Spam.

"Mom, are we really going to eat this?" Bryna whispers.

"I think it would be rude not to." I laugh.

"It looks funny, and what was with that jelly stuff that was all over it when I took it out of the pan?"

Flynn and I are laughing uncontrollably at this point. The look on her face as she looks and sniffs at the bacon-Spam appetizer she has picked up is priceless.

When she finally takes a tiny bite, I am surprised when she doesn't immediately spit it out. After a second of chewing, she pops the rest into her mouth.

"Dang, this is pretty good," she blurts.

"Oh, honey. You didn't think ole Chef would steer you wrong did you?" Chef responds as he squeezes in to take a few pieces for himself.

The rest of the class was full of fun and laughter. We created six Spam-inspired items. Some I wouldn't mind making again at home. The others, well, let's just say I will have to find a way to apologize to my taste buds later.

When class is finished and all the food was packaged up for us to take home, we pose for a quick picture with Chef. He gives us each a hug and tells us that he wants to see us back sometime. He offered to create a whole new Spam menu for us.

After putting our food in the car, I invite Bryna to help me find the perfect spot for the piece of Dad's mug. She smiled and started looking around. Flynn disappeared for a moment and returned with a garden spade.

"Thought you might need this, the ground is pretty solid."

"Thank you, I didn't even think about that."

"I found a spot," Bryna yells.

I turn to see her standing near a small tree. It looks so sad with all its leaves gone. Flynn and I walk over and Bryna and I do our best to dig a small hole.

It took some muscle, but we were able to get a hole big enough for the small piece.

"Good idea with the garden spade," I say as I hand the spade back to Flynn.

He gives me a smile and steps back. He starts to walk back to the car to give us privacy, I assume.

"Where are you going?" Bryna asks.

"I thought I would let you and your mom have a few minutes alone.

"No, stay... you are part of this," she tells him.

Flynn looks to me for approval. I give him a nod and a smile, letting him know I wanted him to stay.

Bryna says a few words and places the glass in the hole and covers it. As she stands, she wipes away the few tears that have escaped. When we get home, I follow my new routine and pull the list out and let her cross the item off the list.

Take a cooking class

Chapter Fourteen
Thanksgiving

The next morning, Bryna and I are up early prepping for our big Thanksgiving feast. I may have gone a little overboard on the invites. Let's see—my mom, dad, Abby, Dave, Casey, Chuck, Leo, Flynn, Bryna, me, and Jack's parents said they *might* stop by. Yikes, twelve people. I sure hope this damn turkey is big enough.

"Bryna, I need you to bring all the chairs from the dining room into the living room," I yell.

"Yes, Mom, I know. You already told me three times."

"Okay, okay. I just want everything set up before we go."

"Mom, it will be fine," Bryna assures me.

An hour later, we have everything set. The turkey is cooking away in the oven, and the table is set up for the buffet style dinner I am doing since space is limited.

"Mom, are you sure you want to go today? We can go later or tomorrow if you want," Bryna asks.

"No, I want to go before dinner. I know that I will be exhausted and then I will feel guilty for not going sooner."

"I think Dad would understand."

"I know, and he is probably up there laughing at my neurotic behavior, and I don't care."

After finishing a few final touches and packing my small bag for our visit, Bryna and I jump in the car and head toward the cemetery. Along the way, Bryna and I make a pit stop at the neighborhood florist, who lucky for us is open until noon today. With all my prep work for today, I completely forget to pick up flowers for Jack. Not that he would actually care, he was never a flower type of guy. Yes, he brought home a bouquet from time to time, but only because he knew I loved getting them.

The cemetery is busier than it usually is when I come to visit. I suppose it is the holidays that bring people out. Everyone misses their loved ones a little more when the calendar makes you take a break from the normal day to day routines and reminds us the loved ones we once shared these days with are no longer with us.

I park the car down the hill from where Jack lay. Bryna grabs my hand and squeezes, letting me know she is here.

"You ready?" I ask.

"Ready when you are." She smiles.

I take a deep breath and open my car door. I grab the flowers from the backseat and we walk up the small hill.

As we approach his headstone, I watch Bryna wipe away a few tears. This is about the time I would normally start crying, but I think I have become so used to this walk that my tears are easier to hold back.

I'm a little curious when I see a card next to his headstone. I look to Bryna to see if she was the one who left the card. She shakes her head no. When we approach the headstone, I once again read the words I chose to sit alongside his name and dates.

HERE LIES A GRATEFUL SON,
LOVING HUSBAND,
PROUD FATHER, AND CARING FRIEND...
WE WILL HOLD DEAR OUR MEMORIES OF HIM,
HIS SMILE, AND THE SOUND OF HIS
LAUGHTER... FOREVER.
AND FOREVER HE WILL BE MISSED.

I kneel down and place the flowers in front of the marble stone and pick up the envelope. Simple block handwriting spells "Mrs. Jack Reynolds." I look around to see if anyone is watching from afar, but I don't see anything out of the ordinary. No one is lurking behind a tree or waiting in a car to see my reaction.

"Who do you think it is from?" Bryna asks.

"I have no idea?" I respond as I rip open the envelope.

It is a sympathy card. The front is a basic fall pattern with gold and yellow leaves. The words "Our thoughts and prayers are with you today" are arranged in large script font. When I open the card more gold leaf designs and the words "Those whom we have loved ever so deeply never really leave us. They live on in our hearts forever." I also see that it is unsigned. Someone left an unsigned sympathy card. Who the hell would do something like that?

As if today was not hard enough, some jackass had to add a mystery to my day. I should be thankful that someone was thoughtful enough to want to leave me a card, but then why not sign it? Deep breath. Inhale. Exhale. Okay, I think rather than losing my shit over a card, I am going to assume that the person that left it forgot to sign it. I'm sure we have all done that before. This could not have been intentional, it had to have been an accident.

After shaking off the weirdness of the unsigned card, Bryna and I spend a little time cleaning up the leaves and old flowers before spreading out a blanket and pulling the Tupperware along with two forks from my bag.

Bryna and I take a seat and prepare to devourer two large pieces of cherry cheesecake. Jack's favorite pie for Thanksgiving was not a traditional pumpkin or apple, or even one of the French silk pie everyone craves. Nope, it was plain old cherry cheesecake, and he didn't like to share. I would make a cherry cheesecake just for him for Thanksgiving while Bryna and I got to fight over the pumpkin. He would sit at the table with the whole tin and slowly eat bite after bite until it was gone in one sitting. He didn't want to take the chance that one of us would sneak a few bites when he wasn't looking.

"Oh, good idea, Mom!" Bryna shouts when she sees what I have.

"I thought your dad would get a kick out of it." I laugh.

We slowly take bite after bite, enjoying each and every one of them as he would have. Bryna jokingly starts to make the little moaning sounds, but almost loses a cherry when she starts laughing at the memories.

"Mom, when are you going to start dating?"

I nearly choke when the words come flying out of nowhere. My gut reaction is to laugh at her question until I see she is perfectly serious.

"Oh, um. I, ah, hmm, well maybe one day when there are flying cars and a colony on the moon," I joke.

Bryna lets out a small laugh at my attempt at humor.

"No, Mom, seriously. I don't want you to be alone for the rest of your life."

She looks at me with such sorrow it breaks my heart.

"Oh, sweetie. I'm not alone. I have your Aunt Casey, Abby, and Flynn and most importantly, I have you."

"Yeah, but they are all busy with their lives and with me off at school you don't have anyone to come home to."

"Well, honey, even if I were to start dating someone it's not like I would start living with them right away," I point out .

"No, I know, but you know what I mean."

"Yes, sweetie, I do. However, these things take time. I have never considered or thought about being with anyone other than your father. Oh wait, I did daydream about Channing Tatum once. How about Channing Tatum... Can I date him?"

Bryna let out a small laugh, trying to hide her smile peeking out from behind her sad eyes.

"No, you can't. He is already married."

"Damn, then I should just join a convent because he would have been my one and only hope for future happiness." I laugh.

Bryna is not able to hide her smile any longer. I love to see her smile. She has had to deal with so much over the last year and a half. I wish I could take all that pain and worry away and just let her worry about being a young adult and not me.

"Come on, let's get going. People will start arriving soon."

"Okay, but promise me, here in front of Dad that you will not wait forever. It's not like you are super young or anything... if you wait too long, you may only be able to choose from the guys Viagra can't even help."

"Bryna!" I shout, laughing.

"What, it's true... you're approaching that hill everyone talks about, and it's all downhill after that." She laughs loudly.

"My God, you are truly your father's daughter," I tell her.

After folding the blanket and repacking my bag, I kneel down one more time and lay my hand on the cold marble.

"If I didn't know any better, I would think you had put her up to that." I pause and look back at Bryna, who smiles back at me as I continue. "Although, I will make you both this promise. I will always keep you in my heart, and *if* I should find someone worthy of sharing my heart with, I promise I will not turn my back on the possibility of where that could lead."

"Thank you, again for coming," I say as I wave to everyone from the door.

It's about time everyone was on their way. Don't get me wrong, I loved having everyone here, but now I am ready to sit back and relax in my comfortable clothes. Maybe even curl up with a glass of wine and watch a movie.

Bryna left an hour ago to go hang out with some friends before she has to leave again. Ah, the sweet sound of the quiet. You never truly appreciate the quiet until you have had a houseful of people wanting to talk your ear off or offer to help a billion times when you have told them repeatedly that you have everything under control.

I love them all for being here for Bryna and me today and appreciate everything they have done for us since Jack passed. He would be happy to know that we are being well taken care of. My mind is wandering when I hear *CLINK, CLINK* coming from the kitchen.

"Hello?" I call out.

"Yes," a voice calls back.

"Flynn, I thought you left with the rest. You nearly scared me half to death," I say, walking into the kitchen.

"Sorry, I wanted to get some of these dishes done for you."

"You *really* didn't have to do that." I smile as I lean against the doorway.

"I *really* do. In my family, the cook of the Thanksgiving feast does *not* do the dishes."

"Ah, but you let the cook do the dishes the rest of the year."

"Of course. Who wants to do dishes more than once, maybe twice a year?" He laughs and sets the dish he finished drying on the counter.

"Are you heading to your Moms next?" I ask.

"Nah, she has had a long days with my brother and his kids, they have long been in their turkey comas by now. I don't need to wake them."

"You are welcome to stay and have some pie with me... I was just thinking a slice of pumpkin sounds good."

"I don't want to overstay my welcome. I should get going."

"Flynn, you could never overstay your welcome. Stay, have some pie. Unless you think my pie isn't any good."

"If you insist."

"I do."

After grabbing wine, pie, and Reddi-wip, we take a seat on the floor in front of the coffee table and begin digging in. Two hours later, we have devoured one whole pumpkin pie, emptied two and a half bottles of wine, and managed to laugh our way through the evening.

"Flynn, let me ask you a question."

"I told you I'm not gay." He laughs.

"No, I want to know why you are so good to us?"

"I'm not sure what you mean?"

"Well, for as long as I can remember you have always been there to help out."

"I'm a nice guy?"

"You are, but that's not why."

"I guess if I knew what you were talking about..."

"For example, why did you make Jack a partner when you started the company?"

"I don't know what you mean, we started it together."

"Flynn. Jack put up a thousand dollars and you put up the hundred thousand your dad left you when he passed away."

"Yeah, so?"

"You made Jack an even partner with you."

"So."

"Why?"

"I still don't know what you mean."

"The hell you don't," I say as I start getting angry.

"What does it matter now?" he asks with irritation.

"Because Jack always brushed it off when I asked and I've always wanted to know."

"It doesn't really matter does it?"

"It does to me. Why is it such a big secret?"

I'm getting a bit irritated. Why has he turned my simple little question into such a big deal?

"Why does it matter?"

"I don't know why, it just does."

"It shouldn't."

"Look, I know you two were like brothers, but for you to use *all* your inheritance when we had nothing to offer, well, that is just too kind."

"Why is that too kind? I didn't know there was such a thing."

"Because people just don't do that, even for their best friend."

"I do, and besides Jack had the landscaping experience that I didn't."

"Flynn, he didn't have that much experience. Quit stalling and just answer my question, or..."

"Or what?" he says with a smug grin.

I'm not sure if it is the wine, the irritation, or his smug little grin he is wearing, but I pick up the can of Reddi-wip sitting next to the empty pie tin and hold it up.

"What do you think you are going to do with that?" he asks, amused.

"If you don't tell me what I want to know I'm going to cream you," I say and spray a small dab of Reddi-wip in my mouth.

"You don't have the guts."

"Don't I?"

"I don't believe you do," he tells me.

"Are you going to answer my question?"

"Nope."

And with that four-letter word lingering in the air, I give

the can one more good shake and begin spraying Flynn's face, chest, and arms. He sits still and allows me to complete my masterpiece without interruption. Once I have finally run out of Reddi-wip, I sit back to take a look at my work.

"Are you done?" Flynn asks.

"No, I don't think so... You are missing one little thing," I respond.

I jump up and run to the kitchen to retrieve the maraschino cherries I have in the refrigerator. The fridge is so full it takes me a few minutes to find the jar hiding in the back. I should have insisted on everyone taking home more leftovers.

As the thought runs through my head, I can feel eyes burning a hole in the back of my head. I turn right in time to see a large white ball of cream flying toward me.

"Ahhhh, you're gonna pay for that," I tell him.

"Oh, I don't think so," he replies.

I tried to turn back to the fridge for another can of Reddi-wip, but he was too fast and I only manage to knock it off the shelf onto the floor. Flynn grabs me from behind and smears more Reddi-wip all over my face and hair. I wiggle my way out of his hold and scurry toward the can rolling around. Flynn grabs my legs and pulls me toward him away from the can.

I turn toward him and grab a clump of cream resting on his shoulder and smear it all over his face. That distracts him long enough for me to break free and get to the can of Reddi-wip. I pop the top and shake well. Flynn charges me and I once again begin spraying him with the creamy goodness.

There is so much whipped cream on the floor now that you can't tell what color the tile is below us. Flynn is able to get a hold of my arms and with his superior strength, he spins my arm to direct the can nozzle at me and then forces my finger to press down, shooting Reddi-wip directly at me. I wiggle and struggle to get free, but my movements cause us to lose our balance and we tumble to the floor. As I lie on the floor, our laughter can probably be heard in China but I don't care. Reddi-wip is everywhere, my hair, my clothes, up my nose all over the kitchen, but again, I don't care.

"Are you okay?" Flynn asks me between bellows.

"Yep, couldn't be better," I snort back.

I slowly stand up and attempt a victory dance, victory over what I'm not entirely sure, all I know is that I felt like somehow I was the winner of this little battle.

As I attempt to do some sort of leg hop cheerleader type pose as Flynn watches from the floor, I slip again only, this time, I land on top of Flynn.

"Ooooooooh," Flynn blurts as I crash down on him.

"Oh my God, I am so sorry. Are you okay?"

"Oh, sure, perfect," he says with a gasp of air.

"Are you hurt?" I ask, trying to hold back my laugh.

"Just my pride."

"Oh you big baby."

I lean down and kiss him on the cheek. The look in his eyes captures my attention. They are not filled with shock because I have kissed him on the cheeks a thousand times. They are not filled with pain. I have seen this look before, but I'm not sure what it means to him.

Not a word is spoken. We are gazing into each other's eyes for what seems like forever, but could not have been more than a few seconds. I'm not sure what would have been said as Flynn moved closer and then rolled me over onto my back. His eyes never leave mine. He is leaning in toward me, and I can feel the butterflies fluttering about inside me.

"MOM! What the…"

Flynn and I shoot our attention to the doorway where we see a stone-faced Bryna staring down at us.

"Uh, hi sweetie, how was your night?"

"What the heck is going on in here?"

"Well, um, you see, well, Flynn and I, he started it," I say, fumbling my words, then laugh and point toward Flynn.

"The hell I did, you liar. You are the one that decided to

cover me with Reddi-wip in the living room," he says, defending himself

"Only because you were being a pain in my ass..." I laugh.

Bryna pulls out her phone and snaps a few pictures then places it back in her pocket.

"I'm going to bed," Bryna says as she shakes her head and walks away giggling.

Flynn and I turn back to each other for a moment before Flynn stands and helps me to my feet. Not a single word is spoken about what was about to happen and I think I am okay with that.

Chapter Fifteen
Chicken, Beef, & Pudding

It has been nearly three weeks since Thanksgiving, meaning our second Christmas without Jack is just around the corner. The snow outside has been falling for hours and the weatherman says there is no end in sight. They also predict that it is going to get even colder over the next few days. The radio station reminds us to stay warm and not to travel outdoors unless absolutely necessary.

With the town all but shut down, there is not much to do to keep me entertained. I've already cleaned the house from top to bottom, played a few games on my phone, picked up a few books, but wasn't in the mood to read, and verified that there is nothing good on the hundred and fifty channels I currently have.

Boredom is the worst thing in the world. You eat food you don't want, you think about things you have no control over, and then you start getting desperate enough for entertainment that you start counting the hairs on your head. That is until your best friend rings the doorbell and saves you from your own insanity.

"Special delivery for Mrs. Piper Reynolds," Abby announces.

"Special delivery? I thought you were coming to save me from going crazy." I laugh.

"Oh I am, but first this is for you."

I look at the envelope Abby pulls from her pocket and see Jack's handwriting once again. I give Abby an excited smile and grab the white paper from her.

Piper,

Well, you said you have always wanted to take a recipe and make it your own "secret" family recipe, but never wanted to waste all the food. So since Christmas is coming and there are so many in need, here is your chance to cook up a storm and whatever is actually edible we will bring over to the shelter and give some to those in need of a semi-good meal.

So pull out those cookbooks and start cooking until you find something you love. My taste buds will be waiting and willing to taste test anything you make.

Jack

That man cracks me up. How in the heck am I supposed to do this. Sure, every woman wouldn't mind having a recipe to pass on to their children. My grandma passed on her homemade egg noodles on to us, my mom passed on her apple pie recipe with homemade crust, but people don't cook like that anymore. Okay, I've never cooked like that.

"So, you ready to get your apron dirty?" Abby asks.

"I have no idea where I would start?" I laugh.

"For starters, you can start by helping me unload the groceries from the truck."

I look to the driveway and see that Abby is not driving her normal four-door sporty car but Dave's large pickup truck.

"My God, how much did you buy that you needed the truck?" I ask.

"A lot… the bag boy was not pleased with me. But I have the truck because Dave felt more comfortable with me driving that with all this snow," she explains.

"Ah, that's nice of him. Let me get my boots and jacket on."

Abby nods and walks back to the truck to start unloading. It doesn't take too long to unload the insane amount of food she purchased. But when you are planning for every possibility I guess it could have been a lot worse.

"Is anyone else coming to help?" I ask.

"Casey was supposed to come, but for some reason today screams let's go house shopping and she has clients back to back all day."

"What about Flynn?"

"Yeah, I'm not sure what is going on with him. He called me last week and asked if I wanted to join in and then yesterday he calls and says he won't be able to make it today but didn't give a reason."

Things had been weird since Thanksgiving and neither one of us brought it up. We both seem to think it was nothing worth talking about. I brushed it off to the wine and the holiday loneliness. If Bryna hadn't interrupted us, I'm sure it would have been more awkward because I'm not sure I would have stopped him. It would have been a mistake for us to go down that road.

Friends should be very careful when crossing that line because once it is crossed, there is no turning back.

"Earth to Piper."

"Oh, sorry."

"Where were you just then?"

"I, ah, I was wondering about where to begin with all this

food you brought."

"Well, I figured you might feel like that so I brought a few cookbooks also," she tells me.

Abby pulls out several cookbooks from a canvas bag and we begin searching the pages for a recipe to destroy.

Neither one of us can call ourselves a chef in any way, so we have no idea what will enhance a recipe and what will kill one.

We decide to start with a chili recipe since that seemed fairly easy to do and not destroy too much. The recipe called for beef so we start by changing it out for ground turkey. We follow the rest of the recipe as directed. We then split it in two so I can try two separate modifications. The first one we add some liquid smoke flavoring and a can of beer. The second we add taco seasoning and cheddar cheese and crushed corn chips. We pour them into the two crock pots I had and set them to simmer.

"Okay, what next?" Abby asks.

"Well those have to simmer for a few hours, and those are the only crock pots I have."

"How about a muffin or cupcake of some kind so we can use the oven," She suggests

We start flipping through the cookbooks again and find a generic muffin recipe that should be easy to add random things to for flavor.

Abby pours the flour, sugar, baking powder, baking soda, eggs, and salt into the mixer while I rummage through the groceries to find stuff to add.

I decide on banana and bacon for one batch, coconut and rum for another, and for the third we try a white chocolate pudding Abby found, marshmallows, and chocolate chips. It's going to be interesting, to say the least.

After mixing all three batches, we spray the muffin pan and pour the mixtures in. It will take them about a half hour to cook fully.

At this point, I'm ready for wine and another recipe. I

pop open a bottle of Moscato and I page through the cookbooks but nothing grabs me. I want this one to be really good. I then walk over to my recipe box and start flipping through the cards.

"So are we actually going to taste all this stuff?" Abby laughs.

"Sure, why not. We haven't done anything too crazy."

"Well, then you can try your little taco chili mix and the banana and bacon muffins." Abby laughs.

"Oh come on those are not all that bad. There is taco pizza, why not taco chili? And people eat bananas on their French toast and bacon all the time."

"No foods like that should always be separate, they shouldn't even touch on the plate."

I laugh at Abby's food "phobia." For as long as I have known her, she refuses to let her food touch each other on plates or mix in her mouth. She claims it is because each food has a flavor of its own and should be enjoyed on its own. When I point out that most of her food is mixed, for example, lasagna or chicken kiev, she agrees that it is not the same because those are entrees. Things like corn and mashed potatoes, scrambled eggs and hash browns, or bread and gravy because the bread gets soggy should never touch, they are served as separate items. Okay, I might actually agree with her on the last one.

When the timer goes off for the muffins, we pull them out and set them aside to cool. Looking over the mass amount of produce we have, I decide to get goofy and start making random things not following a recipe at all.

Three hours pass before we finally sit down to try some of our work. I dish up small amounts of everything we made. The chili, muffins, bacon-covered apples, veggie based salsa and the fruit based salsa that we added some spices to, the crushed cookie cake and, of course, the chicken noodle soup of my great-great-grandmother's that I decided was due for an update.

Once the dishes are pleasantly displayed on the table, Abby and I pose for a few selfies with the food behind us and then sit down for our taste test. Staring at each item, I'm not sure where to start. Do I go for the sweet or the savory? I look to Abby to gauge her choice but find that she is texting.

"Abby!"

"What?"

"You're not going to make me try all this alone are you? Who are you texting?"

"Well, I was trying to get Flynn to come over, but he says he can't and is being an ass about it. What is his problem anyway?"

I look at Abby, unsure if I should let her in on what happened. It could be the reason he is staying away today or he could actually be working. He does not normally work weekends, but with all the snow he could be shorthanded with the plows.

I must have stared at Abby too long because she is giving me the look. The look that you get when your best friend that you normally confide everything to realizes that you are holding back on something.

"What?" she demands.

"I didn't say anything."

"Exactly, that's the problem. What do you know?"

"It's probably nothing."

"Piper, if you know something."

"I'm overthinking, that's all."

"Tell me."

I know she is going to keep pestering me until I spill the beans and normally I wouldn't hesitate.

"Okay fine, but it stays here. You can't tell anyone."

"Piper!"

"Fine. You know on Thanksgiving after everyone left?"

"Yes."

"Well, Flynn stayed to hang out with me."

"So."

"So, we had a few bottles of wine, and…"

"Oh shit, you guys…. um—"

"God, no, but there was a moment in the kitchen. We were on the floor and, well, nothing happened."

"Why were you on the floor and what didn't happen?"

"We slipped on the whipped cream and he almost kissed me."

"OH MY GOD, Piper that is… that is… Okay, I don't know what that is."

"It's nothing, we didn't kiss, but it's been a little weird since."

"Have you guys talked about it? Did you want him to kiss you?" she asks.

"No we haven't talked about it and I'm sure it was just the wine that went to our heads."

Abby looks at me with this goofy little smile and rather than sit and talk about it all night, I insist again that it was nothing and that I was over thinking it. I finally get her to taste test our creations and to our surprise, most of them turned out good. The taco chili was eatable but I would not choose to eat it again and the veggie salsa could be good with some work. My favorite was by far the muffins and the chicken noodle soup with homemade noodles.

Chapter Sixteen
Cleaning Day

After Abby and I finished cleaning the kitchen and packing up all the food in Tupperware, I sort through the rest of the dry goods so we can donate most of it to the food shelf at the shelter. Once everything is packaged and ready for the shelter, I walk over to the hutch to retrieve my list and piece of the red mug.

My newfound tradition of burying the piece next to a tree does not seem likely for this adventure. I tend to kill houseplants within two to three years so I opt not to bury it in one of my potted plants; I look around and decide to put it in one of the champagne glasses on the hutch.

After putting the bag back in its place, I take a seat at the dining room table. Once again, I scan my list and find what I'm looking for and cross it off.

~~Create a secret family recipe~~

I look over the list again and find another I get to cross off.

~~Have a whipped cream fight~~

Before I have a chance to fold the paper and put it back, Abby grabs it, and the pen from me.

"What are you doing?" I demand.

"I think it is time you also start adding to your list," she says.

"I thought the point was to cross things off." I joke

"Yes, but that doesn't mean you can't add some too."

I watch as she scribbles a few items to the bottom, careful not to let me see what she is writing. Once she is done, she hands the list back.

I give her a dirty look and snatch the paper back from her and read the items she has added.

Go out on a date
Sing Karaoke at a bar
Do something stupid
Forgive
Find Happiness Again

"Abby, seriously?" I ask, giving her a dissatisfied look.

"What? Those are damn good items to have on there."

"So who am I going on a date with and who do I need to forgive?" I ask sarcastically.

"I don't know, I didn't have anyone in mind, I'm only adding the first things that came to mind."

"Pfft, right."

"I do have one thing in mind that you could cross off rather than add," she says shyly.

I think I'm going to regret asking but I do anyway.

"What's that?"

After a short pause, she finally answers me.

"Well, you have to make a difference in someone's life right?"

"And…"

"I was thinking that maybe it might be time to clean out Jack's closet. I mean he has so many suits up there that could be donated, that could help someone get a job, or the coats could help someone stay warm."

I'm shocked by her suggestion. It was not something I thought she would suggest. I can see Casey making the suggestion, but not from Abby. I would have expected something along the lines of going to a male strip club to help the poor strippers pay for college.

I had been thinking lately that it might be time. However, each time I open the closet door to take several items off the hangers, I end up putting them right back. Everything feels like they still belong there waiting for him as if he would walk through the door at any moment wanting one of his comfy tee shirts. I guess having them hanging there gives me some comfort. I know that nothing on that side of the closet will ever be used by Jack again, so why am I hoarding them? I hate to admit it, but Abby is right. It is time to let go of some of Jack's things.

"I'm sorry, did I cross a line?" Abby asks softly when I don't immediately respond.

"No, you didn't. I was thinking about how you might be right. It might be time. I just wasn't sure I wanted to admit it yet," I reply.

"If you're not ready, forget I said anything. It wasn't my place to suggest it. I only thought, you know, sometimes you need to hear things from someone else."

"I know, just give me a few minutes to think about it."

"Piper, if you're not ready, then you're not ready. Don't let me push you."

"I know. Don't worry you're not suggesting anything I haven't been thinking about. I just need a few minutes to let my heart catch up with this."

Abby nods and watches me climb the staircase that will lead me to my bedroom. Deep down I know she is right and that I should consider donating Jack's clothing. It's just a hard thing to actually do when the time comes.

In the few support groups I went to, that seemed to be something a lot of people had a hard time with. Some people hired people to come in and take everything, others never got rid of anything, and their items still hang in the closet as they always did. Listening to the others, I knew I didn't want to leave them there forever and that I did want to do it myself. My only issue was when is the right time.

The counselor would always respond to any question regarding timelines with "When it feels right" I get that everyone is different and that we all do things on our own timeline, but geez, can you give me something. I stopped going once I realized it was pretty much the same conversation each meeting.

By the time my thoughts settle, I am standing in front of the closet door. Like ripping off a Band-Aid, I whip the door open and flip on the light. Jack's clothes on the left, mine on the right.

As I walk into the walk-in closet I run my hands over the neatly hung suit coats, his suit shirts, then his tee shirts. He loved that I organized his shirts by style, but would always give me crap about it.

I laugh at the memory of him calling me crazy and telling me that if I'm not careful with my OCD that I will end up jumping over cracks in the sidewalk while singing "Mary Had A Little Lamb." I would smack him and tell him that was mean and that OCD is a real problem for some people.

I take a deep breath and I can still smell him as if he were standing behind me. He had a few items in his hamper that I have yet to wash. I leave them there and figure when the scent is gone, I will finally get around to washing them. Although the scent had faded, it still finds its way to me.

I take a closer look at the items hanging and select a few that even if I had chosen to do this later, I would still not get rid of. They are nothing special, a few old hooded sweatshirts and a few tee shirts. I take care as I fold each one and set them on the bed.

I return to the closet to select a few items for Bryna. I wonder if I should call her and tell her. I'm not sure I want to burden her with this. She knew it would happen at some point.

After trying to decide what shirts she would want to keep and what she would do with them an idea creeps into my head. I'm not sure I have enough time to have it done, but it's worth a try. I select my top twelve choices for Bryna and then I add one more to the pile. A smile forms as I imagine her face when she sees what I have done because no matter how I imagine it, she is always smiling.

I take one last look at the items that have hung next to mine for as long as I can remember. It seems like I have been in here for an eternity and Abby is probably wondering what I'm doing up here.

Two hours later, Abby and I have boxed up all of Jack's clothes, minus the items I chose to keep. I decided to keep an old jacket for Flynn to have if he wants it. It was Jack's old jean jacket. Flynn used to give Jack so much shit for wearing it and he wore it a lot in high school. I think Flynn will get a kick out of the fact that Jack kept it all these years.

We load the last box into the truck and Abby checks with me one last time to make sure I am okay with this.

I assure her that she did not talk me into this; she only helped me realize what I already knew I needed to do. It was time, and she is right, it is a good way to cross off another item on the list.

When we pull up to the food pantry and shelter, I am feeling even better about doing this. It feels like a weight has been lifted from me.

When we enter the delivery door, there are volunteers

busy doing their assigned jobs. Some are stocking food shelves and others are sorting other clothing they received for donations.

I've never been here before. I fortunately, never had a need for their services and donations that we have made in the past were through fundraisers, never a direct donation that required me to come here.

I'm so busy looking around that I almost didn't hear my name being called.

"Piper?"

I turn toward the man's voice, surprised anyone here knows my name. When I turn, I do not recognize the man. I search my memory, but I am sure I have never met him before.

"Hi," I say with a smile.

"Can I help you with something, Piper?" he asks forcing a smile of his own.

"Um, yes, we have a large donation to make tonight," I tell him, still struggling with who he is.

"Oh, okay. What did you want to donate, money or items?"

"I'm sorry, do we know each other?" I ask.

"No not really. We were in one of the Grieving Loss Meetings together. My name is Kyle."

"Kyle, I am so sorry. I should have known."

"No, I sat in the back, I only remember you because your story hit surprisingly close to home," he explains.

"I am really sorry for your loss."

"Thank you. How are you doing?" he asks.

"I'm doing better. In fact, I have taken a pretty big step tonight."

"Oh?"

"My donation is most of Jack's clothing along with some non-perishables. I do also have some home-cooked meals packaged up if you are allowed to take those," I tell him.

"Wow, that is a big step. Good for you."

"Thank you. I'm just glad that someone will be able to get some use out of them."

"We can certainly use all the donations we can get, let me go get a cart. Oh and we cannot accept the home-cooked meals to distribute, but you are welcome to pass them out," he tells me and then walks off to get a cart.

I turn to go back to the truck and run right into Abby. With the surprise of Kyle knowing who I was, I had forgotten she was here.

"Holy cow, did you see him?" Abby blurts as soon as Kyle is out of hearing range.

"Uh, what are you talking about?" I ask, looking behind me.

"He is a hottie with a side of cake," she points out.

The truth is I hadn't noticed, I was too busy trying to figure out where I knew him from." I look back toward Kyle again. He is taller with dark blonde hair, he has a broad build, and looks like he works out.

"Sure he is good looking, are you looking to trade Dave in?" I tease.

"No for you."

"ME? No, he is not my type."

"You don't even know what your type is these days."

I laugh but she has a point. I haven't ever actually dated. Jack and I met in high school and I hardly consider high school dating practices as real dating experience. All I have known is Jack. What the hell do I know about dating?

"Okay, if you show me what boxes you want me to take I'm happy to unload them for you," Kyle says, walking toward us with a dolly cart.

"Piper can help you while I go pass the meals out," Abby blurts.

"Sure, that works."

I roll my eyes at Abby and she prances off with the box of our creations. She mouths the words, *Just do it* back at me. For someone who was trying not to be pushy about getting rid of clothes, she sure is being pushy about me being *hooked up*.

Kyle and I walk to the parking lot where I open the tailgate and hop into the bed of the truck to push the boxes toward Kyle as he loads them onto the cart.

We work without talking much and for some reason, he seems to avoid eye contact. When I do get a glance, they look kind, as if he wouldn't hurt a fly. Maybe Abby is right, maybe it is time for me to make this step. It's not like I can't back off if I'm not ready. If anyone would understand, Kyle would. Ah, what the hell.

"So have you started dating yet?" I ask. My question comes out sounding uncaring rather than the cute, probing question I intended it to be. I think I am going to be extremely bad at this.

Kyle stops and looks at me with what seems to be a combination of fear and confusion.

"I'm sorry that came out wrong," I say.

"I see. Because it sounded like you were getting ready to ask me out," he replies.

"That's because I was, but I didn't mean to sound like a bitch while I did it." I laugh.

"That is very sweet of you, but I don't think that would be a good idea."

"Oh. Ok, that's fine. I just thought I would…" I trail off.

I can feel my face turning a thousand different shades of red. Why did I have to listen to Abby? I mean, come on, I am not mentally prepared for something like this. I am a damn idiot.

"No, Piper, I am flattered. I really am. I'm just not ready. I still have some lingering stuff happening with my wife and although I would enjoy grabbing dinner with you sometime, I just don't think it is the right time," he explains.

"I completely understand." I'm still trying to brush off my embarrassment.

Abby returns as we are unloading the last of the boxes

with an inquisitive look on her face. I shake my head no and give her a *bug eyed I will tell you in the truck* look.

Kyle helps me get down from the bed of the truck, shakes my hand, and thanks me again for my donation.

Abby and I quickly jump back in the truck and I punch her in the arm.

"You had me looking like an idiot," I tell her.

"What, how? What did you say?" she demands.

"It's not so much that. He declined."

"What? Not possible, he would be lucky to go out on a date with you. I'm going to go talk to him."

I grab her jacket before she could get out of the truck.

"No, it's not that. He was very kind in telling me that he is not ready to take that step," I tell her.

"Oh. I guess I didn't consider that."

"It's fine. Hey, at least I did it. I guess that is still a big step."

"Right!"

Rae Matthews

Chapter Seventeen
Christmas

Christmas was the one holiday Jack would look forward to each year. He would stay up late and place the gifts from Santa around the tree, fill the stockings, and always ate the cookies and drank the milk.

Even after Bryna realized that Dad was Santa, he would still sneak down and play his part. The year Bryna went off to school, I didn't expect him to keep up the charade, but that Christmas morning I woke to find that Santa had indeed come to visit me.

After having a large Thanksgiving, I am not eager to have a large Christmas. I have planned it to be only Bryna and me, but since she took the week of Thanksgiving off of work, Bryna won't be here until early Christmas morning. I could tell she was upset that I would be alone for Christmas Eve, but I assured her that I would be just fine on my own.

When I wake up Christmas Eve morning ready to start the day, I have more energy than normal. I am normally not a morning person, but when my eyes open, I am up and ready to start the day. I am not sure if it is the excitement of prepping for tomorrow morning or the chill in the air.

I waste no time getting into the shower and getting ready to go to the grocery store. I planned to make a small ham, mashed potatoes, several finger foods, and a few pies. I cannot forget the chips and dip along with the assorted candies. I plan to have a Christmas movie marathon of old Christmas movies and we will need plenty of snack food.

I also need to make a stop to pick up one of Bryna's gifts. I was nervous it wouldn't be done in time. Though, the ladies at the shop assured me they would do everything they could to get it done in time. I was happy when one of the women called me last night to tell me the final touches were being put on it and would be ready in the morning.

After my morning coffee, I press the remote start on my key fob to let my car warm up while I get my boots and jacket on. I open my front door and cold air washes over me. I take a deep breath and the cold air fills my lungs. Yep, it's Christmas.

The tree limbs and roads are blanketed with a light covering of fresh snow that gives my drive a very magical feeling. I have always loved this time of year—the snow and good cheer makes Christmas special. However, come December twenty-sixth I am ready for summer. I think that cold and snow should start the day after Thanksgiving and end the day after Christmas.

Pulling up to the Pointed Needle Shoppe, butterflies are fluttering in my stomach. I can't wait to see what they were able to do for me.

When I open the door, a little bell rings, letting the clerk know there is a customer. Molly turns to greet me.

"Hello, Piper."

"Hello, Molly. Dorothy called last night to let me know it was ready for pick up."

"Yes it is, let me go get it. I think you will be pleased." She smiles and retreats to the back area.

Looking around the shop, I am still in awe at what these

women can do with a needle and thread. The works of art from cross-stitching to quilting is simply amazing. The little details that they are able to work into each item is mind-blowing, and something I could never do.

"Here you are, Piper," Molly calls to me.

She spreads my project out on the counter and as I look at what they have been able to design and make for me in such a short time, it brings me to tears.

"It's beautiful," I manage to tell her.

"I'm glad you like it, the girls will be thrilled to hear that," she tells me.

"Molly, like is not the right word. Love may not even be a strong enough word to express my feelings," I say, wiping a tear from my cheek.

"Oh, honey, it was our pleasure. We could see how much this meant to you."

"I think my daughter will cherish this forever."

I don't think I will ever be able to top this gift. I know Bryna will be overjoyed and I cannot wait to see her face when she opens it. Next I am off to the grocery store to complete my shopping.

Normally I would never wait until the last minute to avoid the crowds. However, I knew I would need to kill time today. I'm pleasantly surprised that the parking lot is not as full as I expected and manage to get a spot close to the door.

The Christmas music playing over the store speakers puts a smile on my face and I start to sing along as I pick up the items from my list. I offer a smile to those that are brave enough to make eye contact with the crazy lady singing, but to my surprise, most start to sing along briefly as they pass by me. If this was a movie, this is where we would all break out into a dance where everyone is perfectly choreographed. Thank God this is not a movie.

I'm not sure why I am so giddy, I feel alive and ready to take on the world. I suppose I could chalk it up to my excitement about Bryna's gift, but it feels like it is more than that and I want to share it with the world. Hence the singing and smiling to complete strangers. I'm entering the frozen food section when I see a face I recognize. He is staring blankly into the freezer holding the frozen ready-made pies.

"Kyle?"

He turns his attention away from the frozen pies to see who has called his name.

"Piper, hi," he says, shocked to see me.

"How are you doing?" I ask.

"Not too bad. Funny running into you here."

"No kidding. What are you doing for the holidays?" I ask, making idle conversation.

"I'm heading over to my in-laws. They invited me knowing my parents moved to Florida a few years ago."

"That was nice of them."

"Yeah, but they told me to bring a pie and I'm having a hard time picking one out."

"If I can give you some advice, the pies in the bakery are much better, and taste more homemade," I whisper as if it was a giant secret.

"Of course they are better. I don't know why I thought a frozen one would be better." He smiles.

"Because you're a man," I joke.

"Oh sure, blame it on the gender." He chuckles.

"Well, Jack read some article about how some frozen foods might be better for you so he assumed *all* frozen foods were then better. It actually meant he was too lazy to cook when I wasn't home to do it for him," I explain.

"My wife used to do all the cooking. I admit I have put on a few pounds and the pizza delivery guy is paying his way through college off my tips," he says, smiling.

"Oh, I'm sorry I didn't mean to…"

"You're fine. Thank you for the pie tip."

I can see the sadness in his eyes and he almost looks lost. I feel his pain and wish I could do something to help.

"Hey, are you okay?" I ask.

"Yes."

"Because you don't seem like you are okay."

"I'm fine. It's just the holidays. I thought this year would be better..."

"Do you want to go somewhere and talk?"

"No, it's Christmas Eve, and I'm sure you have your daughter waiting for you," he tells me.

I am a little surprised he knows I have a daughter. I do not remember ever talking about her in any of the group sessions, but I must have.

"Actually, she won't be here until tomorrow, so I'm all yours if you need someone to talk to," I tell him.

I can see him contemplating and that he wants to say yes, but something is pulling him toward no.

"Come on. There is a coffee shop around the corner, we can go over there and we can just sit and talk."

"That would be nice," he tells me.

"I'm telling you, she really thought there was such a thing as mini popcorn kernels in the mini microwave popcorn bags and that is why the bags were smaller." He laughs.

I'm laughing so hard that we are starting to get looks from other customers.

"Oh, she sounds like she was a wonderful woman," I tell him as I calm myself.

"She really was," he agrees.

"I'm sorry I won't get a chance to meet her."

"I think she would have liked you," he tells me as his gaze turns to his empty coffee cup.

"I think had I met her, she and I could have been good friends."

Kyle seemed to pull back into himself for a moment before responding.

"Can I ask you a question?"

"Of course."

"How do you deal with the anger?" he asked.

"I'm not sure what you mean."

"I mean how do you move on past the anger that Jack is gone, or the hate you must feel for the woman that caused his death."

I was a little shocked by his question as he and I had spent most of the day sitting in the coffee shop sharing stories about Jack and his wife. We never went into the details of how they died. Kyle didn't seem to want to say her name, I assumed it was some type of coping mechanism so I didn't ask.

"To tell you the truth, I never dealt with that part of it. It's still here festering inside me," I admit.

I don't think that is what he expected from me. He had been avoiding eye contact until my confession. But then again, I didn't expect me to say it. It's not something I had yet admitted to myself.

"You could have fooled me, you seem so happy," he tells me.

"Well, I am happy. I'm happy that Bryna is still in school and that she did not shut down, I am happy that I have my sister and friends in my life, I am happy for the time I had with Jack. The anger lies beneath my happiness," I explain.

"Does it ever take over?" he asks.

"Sometimes," I tell him.

"So how do you control it?"

Now I have a choice—do I let him in on the secret I haven't been able to confess to anyone else or do I keep it hidden away? I'm not sure it would help him in any way. I'm not sure it helps me or if it is the illusion that keeps me returning to the hospital.

If I choose to tell him, will he think me a nut case? Will he think less of me?

In the end, I choose not to tell him. It's not a secret I am ready to part with just yet. Maybe one day I will share it with him or someone else, and even though I have not been to the hospital in months, sitting here thinking about it makes me want to go again.

"Lots of ways. I reach out to my friends or my daughter. I remember the good times we had."

I want to ask him what happened, I want to help him, I just don't know how. He doesn't say anything for a long time. I do not try to break the silence, I will let him when he is ready.

"Do you hate her family?" he finally asks.

"Why would I hate her family? I don't believe I have a reason to."

"I'm sure you do, you just don't know it. I envy you for that."

My heart breaks for him, there is obviously a long and complicated story about the death of his wife. I want to ask him what happened, what is it that keeps him so angry. Maybe I can help, but before I get that chance he interrupts my thoughts.

"I should get going," he tells me.

"So soon?" I joke, attempting to lighten the mood a little.

"You have wasted enough of your time on me."

"Kyle, it wasn't a waste of my time. I enjoyed your company," I assure him as I lay my hand on his. "Let me give you my number. Just in case you need someone to talk to," I add.

He offers a small smile and again I see the same struggle I saw in the grocery store.

"You don't have you use it if you don't want to, but you will have it in case you do." I smile.

"Thank you that would be great," he says.

Kyle walks me back to my car as a gentleman would do and tells me to drive safe. I do the same and wave as I drive away.

I cannot stop thinking about Kyle on the way home. His

sadness runs deep and I am not sure how to help him. I feel bad for him. He seems to be taking her death hard, harder than I have ever seen anyone take a death of a loved one before. I am actually starting to wonder if there is something wrong with me. Should I still be that sad? Should I still be wandering around as I did those first few months? Should I be this happy?

I suppose those are the same questions everyone who has lost a loved one asks themselves. When is it too soon to start living again?

With my thoughts running between Jack and Kyle and how I should be feeling, the drive home seemed to take only a moment. I quickly unload the groceries from my car and start prepping our meal for tomorrow. I want the ham to marinate in the honey brine overnight and I want to get some of the snacks ready for the oven in the morning.

Next, I wrap Bryna's gifts and place them under the tree then carefully fill her stocking. I go ahead and put a few wrapped items in my own stocking for giggles.

After everything is set, I plug in the Christmas tree lights and curl up on the couch to watch *Scrooged*, one of my all-time favorite Christmas movies that I know Bryna will not want to watch.

Bill Murray is about to the meet the ghost of Christmas Present when I feel my eyes getting heavy. I think to myself that I should get my ass off the couch and head up to my bed, but I am *so* incredibly comfortable right here.

I realize that I had fallen asleep on the couch when I am woken by the sound of the floorboard creaking. My first instinct is to jump up and see what or who caused the noise, however, reason takes over and I stay quiet and listen. I almost convince myself that it could be my imagination after not hearing anything for what seemed like an eternity, that is until I hear it again.

I peek open one eye and see that it is still dark out and quickly close it again. My heart is pounding so hard I think it will leap from my cheat, but I manage to listen as I take slow, deep breaths, making it look like I am still sleeping.

CREEEEEEEK

CREEEEEEEK

Okay, someone is definitely in my house. Judging by the direction of the creek, he or she must be close—by the tree would be my best guess. I open my eyes just a sliver to see if I can see anything and manage to make out a shape of a person hunched over the gifts. It is the shape of a man and he is wearing a dark jacket.

What do I do? Do I lie here and hope he leaves? Do I jump up and scream? My phone is in front of me on the coffee table. Do I risk trying to grab it to call the police?

My questions are soon answered when I feel him next to me. I can feel him watching me. When he moves the blanket that was laying next to my legs, my primal need to survive kicks in and I start thrashing my arms and kicking my legs while screaming.

"Don't touch me. Take whatever you want just don't hurt me. Just leave now and I won't call the police!" I scream

"PIPER. Stop, Piper. It's me, Flynn."

"FLYNN! What in the giant fuck are you doing here?"

"I'm sorry. You looked cold. I was only going to cover you up before I left."

"Fine, but what are you doing here, in my house, in the middle of the night?"

"I was hoping to be in and out, I wanted to drop off a few gifts for you and Bryna."

"You almost gave me a fucking heart attack," I scold him

"I'm sorry, I thought you would be asleep in your room, not on the couch. I thought that I could sneak in and out without you knowing."

"Why didn't you just bring them over tomorrow, you know during the day when I would be, you know, awake?"

"Because I thought it would be fun to play Santa for you guys this year."

I pause at his words. If it wasn't such a sweet idea, I would kill him for scaring the living shit out of me. It took me months to get used to the idea of being home alone every night, then a few more months to clear the thoughts of being robbed in the middle of the night without being able to protect myself.

"Okay, that was sweet of you, but next time you decide to break into my house in the middle of the night let me know." I laugh.

"I know, I'm sorry, I guess I thought..." he trails off.

"Don't worry about it, I'm awake now, do you want some coffee?" I ask.

I could see he was embarrassed and now regretted his sweet intention. I know he meant well, so I suppose I can let him off the hook.

"No, I should go, you should go back to sleep."

"Oh hell, that's not going to happen anytime soon." I smile and toss the blanket back on the couch and I stand up.

"Piper, I am so sorry."

"It's fine, you had good intentions. Although remind me to get my key back from you." I joke.

I walk into the kitchen to make the coffee and see the clock on the microwave 5:37 a.m. I can't remember the last time I was up this early.

I pour the water and beans into the coffee maker and press Start. When I turn around, I see Flynn standing next to the center island and staring at the floor where we almost kissed.

"Is that why you have been so distant lately?" I ask.

"Huh?"

"What's on your mind?"

"Nothing."

"Flynn, since Thanksgiving you have been making excuses not to come over and when you are here you are not yourself. Something is on your mind and I assume it has to do with that night."

"You noticed that huh?"

"Flynn? Really? You were over here every few days to check on me or fix something and then you drop by a few times and make excuses when I invite you over. How was I not going to notice?"

"I'm sorry. I thought you would be more comfortable if I gave you some space."

"Flynn, nothing happened."

"But it almost did and that would have been inappropriate on my part."

I walk around the counter and look deep into his eyes.

"Flynn, you have been such a help to me these past months. Your friendship means the world to me and a little thing like getting drunk and almost kissing me is not going to ruin that," I tell him.

I leave out the part where drunk me actually might have wanted him to kiss me.

"Are you sure?" he asks.

"Yes. Now let it go, nothing happened, it's fine," I tell him.

Flynn gives me a smile and nods.

"Now, if you grab my ass we may have to have some words," I joke.

"Deal," he replies.

As Flynn and I take a seat at the dining room table to chat and drink our coffee, the front door opens and Bryna walks in.

"Merry Christmas," she announces.

"Bryna, what are you doing here so early?" I ask, running to give her a hug

"I don't know. I woke up and couldn't get back to sleep so I thought I would just get in the car and come home," she explains.

"Flynn? What are you doing here?" she asks, walking over to give him a giant hug.

"It's a long story I'm sure your mom will tell you later," he tells her.

"Well, Merry Christmas. You are going to stay right?"

"Actually, I should get going."

"No, stay. I have a gift for you."

"No, I will let you and your mom get some sleep."

"Pretty pllllllleeeeeeeeeae stay?" she begs.

"You are more than welcome. I have plenty of food," I tell him.

"Fine. I will stay for a little while."

"Yay! I will go bring my stuff up to my room and then we can open presents and make breakfast."

"Bryna, it's six o'clock in the morning. Don't you want to get some sleep after your drive? We can open gifts when you get up," I ask.

"Um no. The rule is if we are all awake we get to open presents," she reminds me.

"Okay, if that's what you want to do." I laugh.

While Bryna brings her things to her room, I wander back into the kitchen to put the French toast bake I prepared last night into the oven. By the time we are done with gifts, it should be ready to eat.

I hear Bryna and Flynn talking in the living room and when I walk around the corner, I see Bryna now dressed in her pajamas and has already passed out the small number of gifts like she used to do when she was a little girl.

Watching her smile as she shakes the gifts in front of her reminds me of Jack. He used to pick up each gift, shake it, and then try to guess what it was. Granted they were never real guesses because there was no way a Lamborghini or elephant was going to be in the box.

"Okay enough, you don't want to break whatever is in there do you?" I call to her.

"Whatever I can tell it's clothes," she says, shaking the

gift I know is not clothing.

"Well, go ahead and open it," I tell her as I take a seat close by.

Bryna rips open the paper without a second thought and pieces are flying around. She carefully folds open the box flaps. She can see it is not clothing, but I can tell she still has no idea what it is.

Grabbing at the fabric, she carefully removes it from the box and unfolds to see the quilt I had made from her dad's old shirts.

"Oh my God, Mom? Are these... Are these Dad's shirts?" she asks as the tears start to form.

"Yes, honey they are."

She runs her hands over each large square that used to be a tee shirt. She also stops to look at each picture and the little messages that say things like "Daddy's Little Girl" that were stitched in by hand.

"I remember this day," she says as she wipes the tears way and points to a picture that was taken at the zoo about ten years ago. "Oh or this one when we all went to that county fair."

"Do you like it?"

"Mom, I absolutely love it."

As soon as she has finished looking over every inch of the quilt, she dries her eyes and gives me the biggest hug she has ever given me.

"Thank you, Mom, it's perfect. I love you," she whispers in my ear and kisses my cheek.

I can't find the words through my tears so I squeeze her tight.

"Okay, your turn, Mom."

"I think we need to take a break after that one," I joke, wiping the giant waterfall from my face.

"No, we keep going. Here open your gift from Flynn," she says, handing me a small box.

"Ah, mine can wait," he tells us.

"No she can open it now," Bryna tells him.

My curiosity is piqued when Bryna gives him a little look. I have no doubt these two have been conspiring.

When I open the small box, I am amazed to find a necklace, but not just any necklace. It looks like they have taken one of the red coffee mug pieces and placed it in a kind of clear resin. Attached is a small charm that has an image of a coffee mug and reads "Carpe Diem."

My tears are free flowing again as I hold it in my hands, cherishing it. What a wonderful, thoughtful gift this is.

"I hope you don't mind that I stole a piece when you weren't looking," Flynn asks.

"Not at all, I absolutely love it."

"Bryna gave me the idea," he tells me.

I look over to Bryna, who is sporting the biggest smile I have ever seen. She looks so happy at this moment.

"I can't take all the credit. I was on Pinterest and saw something similar."

"I absolutely love it. You could not have thought of a better gift. Thank you," I say again.

I give them both a giant hug and then Bryna helps me put it on. As it rests against my skin, I can almost feel a warmth come over me.

Once our tears are back under control, Bryna hands Flynn a gift to open, but I interrupt.

"Wait. Not that one," I announce.

Neither of them says a word as I stand and walk over to the front closet. I am careful not to let them see what I am grabbing just yet. I fold it neatly over my arm and tell Flynn to close his eyes.

Bryna does a good job of making sure he doesn't cheat and nods when she is convinced he is not peeking.

I turn around and walk back over to where they are sitting. Bryna recognizes what I have and gives me an approving smile.

"I wasn't sure when the right time would be to give this

to you, but I think now is the right moment. Go ahead and open your eyes."

"Ha, Jack still had this." He smiles.

"Yes, it didn't actually fit anymore, but he thought one day he might be able to get it back on," I tell him.

Flynn takes his time looking over the jean jacket that at one time had given him such pleasure in teasing Jack. It was a brotherly like teasing that Jack must have enjoyed since he continued to wear the jacket.

"Are you sure you want to part with this Piper?" Flynn asked.

"I think he would have wanted you to have it," I tell him.

Chapter Eighteen
Baby it's Cold Outside

New Year's Eve, the doorway into the New Year and to new adventures, also known as the last hurrah of the year we are ready to say good-bye to. A day everyone takes a few moments to reflect on the past and ponder future resolutions. A day that we remember those that have entered our lives, but didn't get to stay.

Then there is the kiss. The kiss that sets the tone for the year to come, according to folklore anyway. It is said that the first person you encounter will set the tone for your year. For couples, it will reaffirm their bond to each other while a single person kissing a random loser will suggest a bad year of dating, and should a single person not find someone to kiss as the clock strikes twelve they are destined to have a year of loneliness. It's a good thing I don't believe in folklore, although I do believe in celebrating with friends.

I decided to hire Chef Basil to make us some normal, meaning nonspam, appetizers for me to serve. He, of course, was overjoyed with my request and then offered to drop them off for me.

I, invited everyone. However, since we normally spend every New Year's Eve together, it was kind of a given that they would be at my house anyway. The only difference is that I requested everyone dress in black tie or as close as they could. I wanted to change things up a little this year. I thought it would be fun to say good-bye to such a crazy year in style rather than in our normal blue jeans and sweatshirts. Plus it gives me a reason to wear my dress again.

I may have gone a little overboard with the decorations. Black and silver streamers are draped over anything that would hold it, balloon bouquets in every corner, and those silly little firework centerpiece things all over the table. It kind of looks like Pinterest Decorating 101 threw up in here. I'm putting the final touches on my decorations when Chef Basil knocks on the door.

"Well, hello again, gorgeous," he greets.

"Hello, come on in," I offer.

"Oh honey, have I worked some magic for you," he claims.

I show him to the kitchen where he unloads the first of the four large pans he tells me he has for me.

"Okay, sugar, come over here and take a peek at my masterpiece so I can show you what you need to do," he says, waving me over to him.

"I hope it's foolproof," I tell him.

"Oh, honey. Don't you worry your pretty little head off, a monkey couldn't mess this up."

"You never know with me these days."

"Girly, you are gonna do just fine. Chef Basil hooked you up," he tells me, snapping his fingers.

Chef Basil has to be the only person that I have met that instantly puts a smile on my face. Okay, I have only met him a few times but each time I laughed and smiled uncontrollably from the moment he entered the room. If only he wasn't gay.

He walks me through the effortless instructions for each

pan, kisses me on both cheeks, wishes me a happy New Year during his good-bye and is soon sashaying back to his car. As soon as I shut the front door, I hear my cell phone alert for a text message.

KYLE: Happy New Year, I hope you have a happy evening and that the coming year is better than the last few.

His message is both sweet and sad at the same time. I'm not sure how everyone would feel about this, but I decide to invite him over for the party. Maybe it will remind him there is more to life then grieving for the ones we have lost.

ME: Thank you, same to you. Hey, why don't you come over tonight. I'm having some people over, would love for you to join us.
KYLE: Thank you but I don't want to intrude.
ME: You wouldn't be, just put on black pants and a white shirt and stop over. You don't have to stay if you are not having any fun.
KYLE: I really shouldn't, I just wanted to wish you a happy new year.
ME: If you change your mind we will be at my house until whenever. I would love for you to stop by.
KYLE: Maybe

I figure that is the best I will get out of him and decide not to push anymore. Besides, everyone will be here soon and I still have to change.

With the appetizers safely in the oven warming up, I scoot up to my bedroom to change into my black chiffon dress. I have been looking for a reason to put it on again.

My mind starts to wander back through the year and a half. The last time Jack and I spent New Year's Eve together, we were preparing for a game night with everyone. Casey and Chuck won with Jack and me in a close second.

Last New Year's Eve seems like a blur, a dream even. Bryna came home to "keep an eye on me" since I canceled plans with everyone kind of last minute. I didn't feel like laughing and having a good time without Jack, and I didn't feel as if it was a year worth celebrating, even if it was to say good-bye to the old and hello to the new. Without Jack, it didn't seem to matter anymore.

I'm not saying that this year is any easier to be without him, but I do have to live my life. Jack was my best friend and if he had been looking down, he would be yelling at me and mad that it took his anniversary gift to get me living again. Thank God Flynn decided to execute Jack's master plan. If he hadn't, I would probably be sitting home alone pigging out on some Ben and Jerry's tonight.

I am putting the finishing touches on my makeup when I hear Abby making her presence known as she walks through the front door.

"Holy shit is it freaking cold out," Abby yells as if we were unaware that we live in the Midwest and that it is the middle of winter.

"No shit, Sherlock," I yell back from the top of the stairs.

"Why can't we have a warm New Year's Eve once… I'm not asking for tropical temperatures, but something over ten fucking degrees would be nice." She laughs back.

"I told you I should have taken that job in Florida. We could be driving down to the beach in my new car right now," Dave grumbles at her as he shuts the door behind him.

"Would you drop it already, we are not moving to freaking Florida," Abby replies, giving him a dirty look as she hangs her coat up on the hooks. I watch as she pulls Dave aside to scold him for whatever that was all about. They finish and give me a big smile just in time to greet Casey and Chuck. Casey picks up on the awkward feel in the room and quickly ushers Abby into the kitchen.

"What is going on here?" Casey demands.

"Nothing, it's nothing. Dave is just going through a

midlife crisis. He thinks the job offer he got in Florida is the best thing in the world. He wants to move down there and buy the convertible he has always wanted." She giggles, rolling her eyes.

"Are you guys okay?" I ask.

"We will be fine. He just needs to get that dumb ass idea out of his head," she tells us.

"Well, it wouldn't be New Year's Eve without some whining from Dave." I joke.

When Dave turned thirty, he began realizing that time was moving faster and faster. He would always complain about New Year's Eve—anything from how he has not been able to find a comfortable pair of jeans ever since the new styles came out, to how each year our taxes are going up. Jack and I would bet on the topic each year. I had not given this little tradition much thought until now. I let out a small smile thinking that Jack is probably here with us laughing.

It does not take long for the wine to be poured and the fun to begin. Flynn arrives fashionably late and blames it on the tie he spent an hour trying to get right. Surprisingly, everyone played along with my black tie attire. I knew for sure Abby and Casey would, but didn't expect the guys to show up in full tuxedos.

By eleven o'clock, we are all heavily intoxicated. Not in an *over the toilet bowl praying to the gods that you will never do this again* way. We are at the *no one is driving home, every little thing is funny as hell so we are having a giggle fest* kind of way. What we were laughing at so hard I can't even recall, but I do remember that it all came to a screaming halt when the doorbell rang at about eleven forty-five.

"I'll get it!" I yell, dashing for the door.

I open the door and squeal like a little piggy when I see Kyle standing in front of me.

"KYLE, you came!" I yell, falling into him, trying to give him a welcome hug.

He returns my awkwardly executed hug with a crooked smile then gently helps me to stand up straight again.

"Hey everyone, this is Kyle," I shout with a hint of drunk in my tone as I pull Kyle into the dining room.

Everyone acknowledges Kyle warmly, that is everyone except Flynn. I was a little too drunk to fully comprehend Flynn's reaction, but Kyle understood it.

"You know, this was a bad idea. I should get going," Kyle says as he heads back to the door.

"No, what are you talking about? You're fine," I tell him as I shove a drink into his hand.

"No, really."

"No! You need to drink."

He purses his lips as he holds back his next attempt to argue with drunk Piper. Rolling his eyes and shaking his head, he finally takes a sip of whatever drink I attempted to make for him. Too bad, it wasn't a good drink. As fast as it passed his lips and touched his taste buds, it was ten times faster coming out, spraying all over the table in front of him. The shock of experiencing, what I'm sure was the worst drink he had ever had, was so much for him, that he ending up spilling the rest of it down the front of his shirt.

"Oh, I'm sorry, too strong?" I ask while not doing a very good job of holding back my laughter.

"Not at all, I just wasn't ready for... whatever that is," he says.

I watch as he tries to pull his wet shirt away from the skin on his chest while looking around as if he isn't sure where to go next.

"Ten, nine, eight..." Abby starts shouting without warning.

Realizing the clock is about to strike midnight we all jump in, well most of us.

"Seven, six, five, four, three, two, ONE!"

Everyone cheers then the kissing starts. Without thinking, I lean into Kyle and lay a sweet, innocent, no tongue kiss on him. The look on his face is priceless, at least what I saw of it anyway. His eyes are bug-eyed and his lips look as hard as they were when I felt them on mine.

Before I can say a word, I am pulled from him, and spun around faster than my stomach would have liked.

When my eyes decide to focus, I see Flynn with a not so happy face. I think he needs a kiss too. Everyone should be kissed on New Year's Eve.

I throw my hands around Flynn's neck, pull him closer, and press my lips to his. For a quick moment, our lips are locked together and it felt nice. When I finally pull away, I see yet another shocked face. However, his eyes are not bug-eyed, they are more confused, irritated, deer in the headlight, but I'm too drunk to give a crap. All I actually cared about was that his lips were soft and didn't pucker in protest like Kyle's had.

My stomach catches up with the spin from a moment ago and I feel a little woozy. My eyes can't seem to focus on any one thing in the room.

"Here sit," Flynn tells me, moving me toward a chair.

My head bobbles around still trying to focus when I see Kyle. Oh poor Kyle, he is still standing there with his wet shirt.

"Oh, you look, un, not happy," I stutter.

"Yeah, um, do you mind if I clean up a little bit."

"The kitchen is through that door. Let me get you a towel…" I say as I start to stand.

"I got him," Flynn offers, quickly putting his hand on my shoulder.

A second later, Flynn is escorting Kyle to the kitchen. I have no choice but to lay my head back on the wall and close my eyes. Tomorrow I am so going to be mad at myself for tonight. I honestly cannot remember the last time I drank this much. I think I am in desperate need of hydration.

"Water," I whisper.

No one hears me.

"Can someone get me some water," I say a little louder.

No point, everyone is too busy laughing and being crazy. They are about as drunk as I am.

"Okay I will get it myself," I mutter.

I feel like the world is attached to my feet as I stand and start to make my way to the kitchen. I start giving my feet a countdown of the number of steps they have to make.

"Two more steps, you can do it," I tell them as I cling to the wall for support.

Two steps later.

"Oops, I lied you have two, um, maybe three," I clarify with a giggle.

Four steps later.

"See, I knew you could do it. Now take me to the sink. Just two more, wait I mean right more, I mean… " I tell them as I approach the doorway.

"You can't even look me in the eyes and tell me that, can you?"

Huh? Feet don't have eyes and feet cannot talk. Wait, that was Flynn.

"Look, there is nothing happening. She invited me over and it was obviously a mistake that I stopped by. As soon as I'm done here I will leave," Kyle responds.

"She has no idea who you are does she?" Flynn demands.

My feet are frozen in place. Am I drunk dreaming? How does Flynn know Kyle? What does he mean, do I know who he is. I'm so confused.

"It hasn't come up… I keep trying to tell her, but I don't want, I can't, I will… I swear," Kyle answers.

"You stay away from her. This, whatever this is, ends tonight," Flynn tells him.

"I swear, we are friends. Nothing more."

"Only because she is clueless as to who you are."

"Look, I tried to stay away from her. She kept being so… so nice."

"You tell her who you are or I will. Then she won't ever

want to see you again."

Flynn gives the last word and bumps into me as he makes his exit from the conversation.

"Piper, hey, sorry. You okay?" he asks.

"Yep, just dandy," I answer.

"You should be sitting down," he tells me.

"I needed water."

"You should have yelled for me."

"I tried you were too busy yelling at Kyle," I tell him.

Flynn giving me a mad-eyed look, bites his lower lip in frustration. It makes me wonder even more what the hell that argument was all about. Who is Kyle? I thought I knew Kyle? How does Flynn know Kyle?

"So, you don't like Kyle, huh?" I blurt.

"I think he owes you the truth, that's all."

"KYLE, what's the truth?" I shout playfully toward the kitchen.

Everyone stops what they are doing to turn their confused attention toward me.

"TRUTH OR DARE! YEAH!!" Abby shouts with excitement.

"Not tonight, Piper. Kyle was just leaving and you should probably head up to bed," Flynn tells me.

"Oh come on, I want in on the secret. I can keep secrets. I have secrets," I ramble.

"No, not tonight. Come on let's go get you to bed."

"You are no fun. Kyle doesn't have to leave, he just got here. Come on let me in on your little secret?" I beg.

"Piper, not tonight. Kyle will call you tomorrow," he says then shoots Kyle a dirty look.

Kyle shakes his head yes then avoids my eyes by looking at the floor. When I look back to Flynn my eyes fail me. I am now seeing double and find it extremely hard to focus.

"Fine! But only because there are two of you and I can't take both of you. One sure but not two," I agree.

Flynn gives me a small smile as I turn to walk toward the

staircase and stumble. It was only a little stumble and it only happened because I couldn't feel my feet anymore, but Flynn took that to mean I was unable to walk. Flynn scooped me into his arms with little effort.

"Good night to you all, I thank you for coming but now I must sleep. Feel free to party on in my absence!" I tell everyone as Flynn carries me toward the staircase.

Everyone laughs. I caught a glimpse of Abby holding up her cell phone, no doubt there will be several videos of this evening to prove exactly how drunk I was.

As Flynn takes the first step up the staircase, I give in to the comfort of his arms. I lay my head on his shoulder and take a deep breath. I can't help but take in his scent. God, he smells good. I cannot pinpoint the cologne, but it is very cool and sweet with a very masculine undertone.

Flynn reaches my bed and gently pulls the comforter down then lays me down. I reluctantly let go of his neck. His embrace was intoxicating. I didn't want to let him go. This was the first time I have been in a man's arms since Jack. I forgot how much I missed feeling that kind of warmth.

I'm not sure if it was the alcohol, the mood, or what that made me grasp Flynn's neck as he bent down to pull the comforter over me. He didn't pull away and I took that as my signal.

I pull him closer to me and touch his lips to mine once again. His lips are soft, so soft. His scent invading me.

"Wait, stop," Flynn says as he pulls away.

"What? Why?"

"Piper, you're drunk."

"Yes I am. Don't you want to take advantage of that?" I smile.

"Not at the expense of our friendship."

"If you were a real friend you would help a friend out. I mean you're a man, I'm a woman, and we can do things and help fill in the holes." I can feel the emotions flooding in as the words come out of me.

"Piper, doing this isn't going to fill any holes, and you will regret it in the morning," Flynn tells me as he caresses my cheek.

"I just miss this so much. Having someone to hold and keep me warm. To know that there is someone else to take care of me and me to take care of them..." I trail off with the tears start to flow.

"I know, we all miss him."

"Can you stay with me, hold me, nothing more."

Flynn doesn't say a word. He stands to take off his shoes and jacket. He turns off the light and crawls in to bed beside me. A moment later, he pulls me close into his embrace. For the first time in a year and a half, I feel a tranquil bliss fall over me.

Rae Matthews

Chapter Nineteen
Hangovers & Heartache

The morning creeps up on me. I feel like I just fell asleep yet the sun is up. Looking to the windows, the bright light forces me to close my eyes.

"Oh my God," I whisper to myself.

My head is pounding and my eyes scream at me each time I open them. What the hell did I drink last night and how much did I have?

"Kill me, kill me now."

"Sure. How do you want me to do it."

I jump at the sound of Flynn's voice. My eyes pop open and I see him standing in the doorway holding two coffee cups.

"Flynn! You scared the shit out of me," I yell, grabbing my head when it starts vibrating with the sound of my voice.

"Sorry, I thought you would be in need of some coffee when you woke up," he tells me as he crosses the room toward me.

When he hands me the warm mug filled with the brown liquid of life I so desire right now, a foggy memory comes to me.

I look into his eyes for any sign that the memory is real. As far as I can tell, he seems completely normal. No signs of weirdness or confusion that would certainly be there if we had, in fact, kissed and then spooned all night long.

Flynn is sitting quietly sipping his coffee. He is giving me the silence he knows I need to allow my hung-over brain to wake up. The more I look at him, the more comes back to me. A fight, no not a fight, an argument. An argument with Kyle.

"Your memory starting to catch up with you?" Flynn asks.

"Um, yes. But I'm not sure if it is a memory or a dream... did we... kiss?"

"Twice." Flynn smiles.

"Oh God, I'm sorry. I was *sloppy drunk make out girl* last night, wasn't I?" I cringe as I ask.

"No, not really. You kissed me at midnight and then again when I put you to bed."

"I am so sorry Flynn, I'm mortified."

"Nah, don't worry about it. I think the begging to spoon with me was the real low point of the evening for you." He chuckles.

"Are you kidding me right now? I spooned you?"

"No, no, I was the big spoon." He smiles and takes another sip of coffee.

The memory of feeling desperate to be held rushes over me. In all the time that Jack has been gone, and all the times I have wished to be able to touch him again, I had never felt the need for a man's touch that strongly until last night. I could brush it off to my blood alcohol level or that it was New Year's Eve but I have a strange feeling that it is more than that. No, I cannot let my brain go there right now. It will take way more brainpower than I am able to give at this particular moment.

"Flynn...I..." I start.

"Don't worry about it, it's fine. We all have those nights," he says, smiling.

"But, I…"

"No need to talk it out, its fine…"

"Okay, but I do have another question."

He doesn't respond with words. His body tightens up, his face turns hard, and there is a hint of anger in his eyes.

Wow, I don't ever remember seeing him like this. Yes, I have seen him mad and pissed off, but this is a whole new level.

"Um, I'm going to guess by your reaction that you already know that I am going to ask if there was something going on with Kyle last night," I tell him.

"Yes, I think it would be a good idea if you didn't see him again," he tells me sternly.

"Okay, can you tell me why?" I ask.

"It's not up to me to tell you. He should have told you the moment you met."

"So why don't you tell me."

"Because I think he needs to take responsibility for his deceit."

"My God, Flynn. What is going on? Who is he?" I demand.

"Piper, that is a conversation you will need to have with him. He said he would call you later today and I will give him today. If he fails, then his secret is mine to tell you tomorrow."

"Secret? Flynn, what the hell?"

"I'm sorry, Piper, you need to talk to Kyle."

I can see in his eyes this conversation is going nowhere fast. He has made up his mind and that was the end of that story.

"I should get going," Flynn tells me.

"Are you sure?" I ask. Although he isn't giving me any answers, it is always nice to have him here.

"Yes, I'm going to head out. I could use a change of

clothes." He smiles, pulling at his extremely wrinkled dress shirt

"I suppose I could use a long shower myself."

Flynn walks over to the chair in the corner and grabs his suit jacket and shoes. He offers a smile as he leaves the room. A few moments later I hear the front door close and I am once again alone.

A few hours later, I am showered and my tummy is full of greasy bacon and eggs, 'cause that always helps with a hangover for some reason. Next on my list is to clean the house. We are not super messy party people like we were fifteen years ago and it looks like Abby and Casey must have done a once-over before they left, thankfully.

I'm about to dive in when my cell phone rings. I look at the display and see it is Kyle. I thought about calling him the moment Flynn left, but given my head was going to explode, I decided to wait and see if he called.

"Hello."

"Hi, how are you feeling?" Kyle asks.

"I'm not going to lie, it's been a pretty rough morning."

"I bet it has been, do you remember much of last night?'

"Not in great detail but I do have some flashes."

"Oh, so you do remember…"

"Yes, I remember you seem to have something to tell me about who you are and why I shouldn't be hanging around you," I interrupt.

Normally I would not be this straightforward. If someone had something to tell me I would let them tell me in their own time, but given Flynn's reaction to Kyle, I don't feel like pussyfooting around the issue today.

There is a long pause. The only reason I know he is still on the line is I can hear his breathing.

"Kyle?"

"I owe you an apology…" he starts.

"Okay, why?"

"I should have told you who I am when we first met. I'm Helen's husband."

My heart stops when I hear the name. The name that instantly makes my skin crawl and my blood scream in my veins. The name that forever changed my life and ripped my happiness away.

"Excuse me?"

"My name is Kyle Warren and Helen Warren was my wife."

"What the hell kind of game are you playing here?" I demand.

"It was no game. I had no intention of ever contacting you, but then you came in while I was working and then one thing led to another, I didn't know how to tell you."

"You didn't know how to tell me? Are you fucking kidding me? How about in the coffee shop when we were talking about her?"

"I didn't know how to…"

"You know, I was starting to feel sorry for you. I felt like we were the same, like we shared something that no one else could. I thought… I thought…" I say, screaming into the phone.

"What? What did you think? And how am I any different than you? We both lost someone we loved." he asks.

His question stops my rage in its tracks. He's right. Why is my loss any more substantial than his is. We both lost someone we loved, should it matter that his wife was the cause?

"You're right, I am sorry. Your pain should be no different than my pain. I should not have implied that your loss was any less than mine," I say softly.

"Thank you, but if I am being honest, my pain is so much more than yours," he tells me calmly.

"How do you mean," I ask, confused.

"Because the accident is all my fault."

The phrase catches me off guard. That was the last thing I would have expected him to say. How could this be all his fault?

"Kyle, she was alone in the car… how could this be your fault?"

"Because she was on her way to see me and she was running late," he tells me.

"I don't see that how that could be your fault. Wives go to visit their husbands all the time. No one can predict these things," I tell him.

"Yes. However, a week before, I asked her for a divorce and she was meeting me for breakfast to talk about reconciliation," he confesses.

My heart breaks for Kyle. He has been carrying this around on his shoulders. This explains a lot about our past conversations.

"Kyle, that still doesn't make this your fault."

"How? If I hadn't been a jackass I wouldn't have left and she wouldn't have been driving to meet me so she wouldn't have been there to kill your husband."

"Kyle. Stop. I know nothing I say will give you any comfort, but you need to stop thinking that. This is not your fault."

"But I still loved her. I didn't want to divorce her, I felt, I wanted, God it's so stupid," he mumbles through his tears.

"I forgive you."

"What? How can you forgive me?"

"Kyle, I will be honest. I am not in a place yet to forgive Helen, and I'm not sure I ever will, but I will never blame you for this. No matter what happened between you two that led her to being there that day, it is not your fault. You did not put the lipstick in her hand and you did not make her hit my husband. You would have no way of knowing that would happen," I tell him.

"But, if I …"

"Kyle, no. I know it will be hard for you but you cannot blame yourself."

"I'm so sorry for my part in your loss. That is why I left the card at Jack's grave, and that is why I tried to stay away from you."

"The card was from you?"

"Yes. I hate that I played any part in your pain."

The dots are finally being connected and it all makes sense. The pain I always saw in his eyes, the brush-offs, the odd way he avoided any details about his wife.

Kyle and I stayed on the phone another hour or so. I think it was helpful for him and in a small way it was helpful for me. In the end, I did let him know that although I still do not blame him, I wasn't sure what kind of friendship we could have, now knowing how we are forever connected. I assured him that if he needed me, I would always be here for him, and that I wished him happiness before telling him good-bye.

I may not be able to forgive Helen for what she has taken from me. Maybe one day I will. However, today is not that day.

I suppose I should be mad that Kyle didn't tell me who he was in the beginning. Who knows, if he had I might not have been able to hear him. I might not have been able to share my grief with him. In a strange way I'm glad I got to know him before I knew who his wife was. Knowing why she was there and knowing a little bit of her story, in a small way, helps. She wasn't just a woman being vain about how she looked for another normal day of work or shopping. She was a woman who was trying to save her marriage.

Chapter Twenty

PIZZA! PZZA! PZZA!

When Flynn gives me the letter for my next adventure, I'm not sure I give him the response he is looking for.

Dear Piper

The weather might be frightful but it will be so delightful as we frolic in the snow. Okay, that is about the best rhyme I can come up with. Today we take a trek up the hill to try your hand at skiing. Now don't be scared, because I will be there, you are going to do just fine.

Flynn

"No way, I'm too old for that!" I tell Flynn.
"Come on, I will be right there."
"I'm going to break something."
"You're right, you will probably break a hip or

something," he jokes.

"Hey, I'm not that freaking old."

"Then stop acting like it and get it the car."

"Fine, let me grab my stuff."

The fresh coat of snow we got last night made today the perfect day for my next adventure. I get to ski. When I was in high school, I used to drive to the ski hill and would imagine how fun it would be to give it a try. Then spring would come, telling me I missed my chance for that season. After Bryna was born, we never had the money or the time to try something so dangerous.

Okay, so it is not super dangerous. Nevertheless, when your bank account is as broke as a twig that Big Foot stepped on and there is a larger potential for a small injury causing an emergency room visit that would add to your already financial strain, things like this no longer become an option.

However, now that those old excuses no longer hold water and since it was on my list, I have no choice but to follow along with this latest insane Carpe Diem adventure.

Waking up three weeks ago to find that I had both kissed Flynn and made him stay to cuddle with me, I would have thought it would make a day like today rather awkward. On the contrary, the drive to the ski hill is filled with teasing digs at one another and we are not holding back.

After talking to Kyle I called Flynn. I finally understood why Flynn reacted the way he did. He was looking out for me. He told me about me kissing Kyle. He had assumed that it meant more than me being drunk. When I explained that we had only been friends and that I ended the friendship, I could hear the relief in his voice. I could tell without a doubt how worried he was and that it weighed heavily on him.

"Okay, you ready for this?" Flynn asks.

"As ready as I will ever be I guess," I answer with hesitation.

"You will do just fine. If you can jump out of a plane,

you can slide down a hill on sticks."

"Yeah, right. We will see about that. At least with the skydiving there was someone attached to me in full control."

We both exit the car and make our way to the warming house to get fitted for our equipment. The area is alive with people. The new snow has them all excited. It's funny to see this many people excited by the weather. I am a summer person and tend to hibernate in the winter like most sane people do from November to March. I love to sit cuddled up in the warmth of my house with a cup of hot cocoa and a good book or movie to keep me company.

We enter the large warming house that is crowded with people warming themselves in between runs down the slopes.

Flynn leads me to the shop where I assume we will pick up our ski equipment. When we enter the shop, it is full of everything you could ever need or want for this insane sport. The back wall is lined with skis and snowboards. The center is filled with jackets, snow pants, and head gear. Other shelves are scattered around with other supplies one would need to hurl themselves safety down a snow-covered hill. Idiots.

As we make our way to the counter, the white-haired man looks up and greets Flynn.

"Mr. Avery, I thought we might see you today," he says.

"We couldn't ask for a better day for a beginner," Flynn responds.

"This must be Piper."

"Yes, hello."

"I'm Henry. It's so nice to meet you. I have heard a lot about you. I hope you enjoy your day on the hill. Let's get you set up."

A short time later, Flynn and I are covered in more gear than I could have ever expected. Between the thermal layer, fleece layer, and the outer layer, I'm surprised I'm able to move. To my surprise, it is actually pretty flexible.

We move over to the ski equipment next and Henry set us up with skis, helmets, goggles, boots, bindings, and poles.

"Okay, you should be all set. Detter should meet you on the bunny hill for your lesson," he tells us and points in the general direction to get us to the bunny hill.

Grabbing our stuff, we head outside and start walking the trail signs that will lead us to the bottom of the bunny hill.

"Detter?" I whisper to Flynn as we walk.

"I guess. I've never met him."

"We are getting lessons from a guy with the name Detter? He sounds like a pothead high school kid." I laugh.

Then I hear a voice from behind me.

"Nah, I always thought hippy lettuce was a waste of time."

I turn to see a very attractive, tall, dark-haired, blue-eyed man. I give him an embarrassed smile and turn back to face Flynn.

"Don't worry, happens all the time. My parents were hippies," he tells us.

"Hello Detter, I'm Flynn and this judgmental ass is Piper," he says, holding back a laugh.

My jaw drops in shock at Flynn's words. In retaliation, I punch him on the arm and give him a dirty look.

"Ow, that hurt," he cries out.

"Oh stop being a baby. I didn't hit you that hard." I laugh.

Detter waits for us to finish our dramatic scene and then leads us toward a conveyor-belt-looking thing that will take us to the top of the small hill. A few feet away, to the right of the belt, is an area people use to get their skis on.

Detter guides us to the "prep area" and has us each set our skis down parallel to each other. After scrapping off some snow on the bottom of our boots, he instructs me on how to attach my boot to the sticks of death, I mean skis.

"Okay, did you hear that click?" he asks.

"Yeah."

"Good. That means you are locked in and ready to go," he tells me.

"Oh goody," I say sarcastically.

"Now, before we go up I want you to get a feel for the weight and the movement of the skis. Go ahead and slide them back and forth. You can also pick them up and move left to right if you feel comfortable," he instructs.

After a few minutes of playing with my balance and trying to get a feel for these things, Detter tells me I'm ready to go up the hill. We make our way to the belt. Flynn goes up first so Detter can help me.

Looking down the hill, it doesn't look too incredibly terrible, and with the number of kids that are going down with no problems at all, my fear subsides a little.

"Now, to start I want you to keep your skis parallel and use your poles to give you a little nudge."

I do as he says and get a gold star for execution.

After about ten minutes of continuing to practice on that, he teaches me how to pizza. A move named because of the pizza slice shape your skis make when you shift the back of your skis inward, forcing the front to spread wide, he explains this is to help me slow down.

Once Detter feels I am ready, my next stop is the bottom of the bunny hill. With both Flynn and Detter close by my side, we slide down the hill at a slow yet steady speed. My heart is pounding. I can feel the adrenaline coursing through me. When we arrive at the bottom of the hill, they each give me a high-five and up the belt we go for another run.

Three hours later, I have a hard time believing I was nervous about this. I graduated to the green hill, and I'm feeling pretty confident at this point and feel I'm ready to try the blue hill.

Flynn and I jump on the lift and wait patiently for our off

point. This has been an awesome way to spend such a wintery day.

We are a few seconds away from getting off the lift when my pole gets caught on something. I'm working fast to try to free it before I can tell Flynn he is hopping off the lift while I am forced to stay on.

"PIPER, WHAT ARE YOU DOING?" he yells to me.

"MY POLE IS STUCK, I WILL RIDE IT BACK AROUND," I yell back.

"NO YOU CAN'T! YOU HAVE TO GET OFF AT THE BLACK DIAMOND, DO NO GO TO THE TOP! WITH OR WITHOUT YOUR POLE GET OFF…" Flynn's voice is getting softer and softer at the end. I can see he is still yelling and pointing but I can no longer make out he is trying to say.

I watch as he turns and starts down the hill. I only have a few moments to try to get my pole lose before I have to get off. Flynn was pretty adamant that I get off on the next hill so I better do what he says.

"Finally!" I yell when I free the pole.

I'm right in time to see the warning sign to prepare to get off the lift at the black diamond. It took a lot longer to get to this next hill then I thought it would.

I glide off the lift and maneuver over to the start point. Looking down the hill from here, I damn near shit my pants.

"You have got to be kidding me," I say to myself.

The hill is much steeper than I thought it would be. The people flying past me from the double black diamond hill above are going at a speed I have not achieved yet.

"I'm going to get killed. No freaking way, I can't do this."

I walk over to the lift attendant. There has got to be another way to get off this damn hill.

"Excuse me? Is there another way of going down the hill?"

"On your skis or on your butt," he tells me as he keeps

his attention on the lifts.

"I'm sorry?'

"Only two ways you can get down from here, on your skis or sliding on your butt," he explains again.

Little shit is no help at all. I know I do not want to be one of "those" people who has to slide down on their ass. Everyone else is doing fine, I'm sure I can do this. I have to do this.

"You know you got this, you can do this," I tell myself.

After my continued pep talk, I reluctantly decide it is time to push off, to meet my possible end.

"One, two, and three..." I count

"PIPER WAIT," Flynn yells from the lift,

It is too late. I have already pushed off and I am on my way down the black diamond hill.

My speed is increasing rapidly. I have to concentrate on keeping my legs loose and my skis parallel. Holy shit I am going so fast. How in the hell do you stop at this speed? I'm gonna die!

"PIPER."

I hear my name behind me but I am too scared to look. Thank God Flynn catches up to me and is beside me in no time.

"I TOLD YOU TO WAIT," he says, scolding me.

"I COULDN'T HEAR YOU AND THEN I SAW YOU GO DOWN THE HILL," I yell back.

We are approaching the bottom. The building that once looked like a little doll house is growing in size much faster that I am used to.

"I NEED YOU TO SLOW DOWN."

"HOW THE HELL DO I DO THAT?'

"PIZZA."

I push out on my skis like I had done before, but my speed doesn't slow as much as I need it to.

"PIZZA, PIZZA," Flynn instructs.

"I'M TRYING," I scream back.

Flynn sees the panic in my eyes and moves to position in front of me as we approach the last stretch to the bottom.

"PIZZA! PIZZA! MORE PIZZA!" Flynn yells one last time.

I push out the back of my skis as hard as I can, my speed finally starts to slow unfortunately not enough.

"Uuuuug."

"Oooooowwww."

"Arrrrh."

"AHHHH."

I slam right into Flynn, who had come to a stop in front of me. We lie on the ground not more than five feet from the wall of the warming house, tangled up in each other.

"So how was it for you," Flynn asks.

"I've had better." I laugh..

Flynn starts to untangle from me when I feel it.

"Ahhhh," I scream.

"What, what is it?" he demands, concerned.

"My knee, it hurts a little," I tell him as I start to give it a rub.

Flynn carefully stands up and unlatches both our skis to avoid causing additional pain to me. He gently helps me stand up, then again with no effort, he scoops me up into his arms.

A few people around us make sure we are okay as he carries me into the warming house. I feel like an idiot. I should have known Flynn would not leave me to fend for myself at the top of a dangerous hill. I should have known that he was going down the hill to get back on the lift to meet me.

Flynn finds an open table and sets me down gently in one of the chairs, then props up my leg with another.

"Try to get your ski pants off while I go get you some ice," Flynn tells me.

"Okay, do you think it's broken?"

"Your knee? No, I think you twisted it, but I will get

some ice and the ski patrol to have a look."

A few minutes later Flynn returns with the ice and a woman from the ski patrol. After a short examination, she determines that I was lucky and only twisted it, and I should stay off it as much as possible. She suggests that if I still have the same level of pain tomorrow I should see my doctor.

"So, not one of my more graceful moments." I laugh.

"I would agree, but I'm glad you are okay."

Flynn lifts my leg just enough to sit in the chair. He then places my foot on his lap. I watch as he begins to massage the muscles around my knee. It hurts, but it is a good hurt like he is working out the knots. I lean my head back, close my eyes, and enjoy as his hands connect with my skin. His hands are still slightly chilled from holding the ice pack he brought back.

When I finally lift my head, I see Flynn's attention is not on my knee but on me. I can feel my cheeks blushing. I can't say that I have ever seen him look at me like this. I cannot explain it.

My heart is starting to race and I feel something I haven't felt in a long time. My core is fluttering and my skin is tingling. What the hell is happening here? Stop it, shake it off. It's Flynn. He is only being a good friend, nothing more.

"So maybe we should get going," I blurt.

"We can do that. I can't imagine you will want to go down another hill today. Even if your knee would allow you to," he says, smiling.

"Yeah, that would be a big fat negative, Ghost Rider." I snort loudly.

"Settle down there, Maverick. Let me go take care of our equipment. You wait here."

I nod and without hesitation, he is off to retrieve our skis and things that we left outside where we fell.

While he is gone, I roll down my pant leg and place the ice pack on my knee. My momentary distraction doesn't last long and my thoughts are brought back to my little moment with Flynn.

Actually, is it a *moment* if he was unaware of the part he played in it? Was this all a product of my adrenaline high coming down? Did I imagine the look in his eyes? I mean it is Flynn, we have been friends for almost twenty-five years. He can't possibly have felt what I felt... could he?

"Okay, you ready?" Flynn asks.

His voice startles me away from my borderline obsessive thoughts.

"Yep. Just have to do one thing before we leave," I tell him.

"I figured. I have the spade right here."
I smile when I see Flynn is holding a little spade shovel to help us bury my red piece of mug.

Chapter Twenty-One
Valentine Schmalintine

Wow, time is flying by as if it is in a race to the finish line—Valentine's Day already. It seems like it was summer only yesterday and I was finding out about this crazy plan Jack had for me.

I can't believe that Jack has been gone almost two years. This is my second Valentine's Day without him. Again, not that we ever made a big deal about the holiday especially since we always had Bryna's birthday on February fourth. What little money we had in the beginning we always spent spoiling our little princess.

When Flynn texted last week letting me know that I have plans for Valentine's Day and not make any, I knew it was the next adventure.

The last few weeks have been filled with thoughts of Flynn. Ever since he dropped me off from our ski adventure, I have been trying to analyze everything he says and does. Is it out of friendship or is there more there?

So far I have been able to convince myself that it is only a figment of my lonely imagination. If I were to try to get all-Freudian on myself, I would have to conclude that between the holidays, my drunken attempt to fill the void I feel, and his heroic actions that saved me from serious injury, I have managed to manifest fake feelings for my dead husband's best friend. Something that is not there and projecting my feeling of gratitude for everything he has done for me into some sort of way.

I have to laugh at myself for all the crazy thoughts that I have allowed my brain to conjure up. If Flynn knew even half of the thoughts I have had about him, he would probably laugh his ass off then have me committed for sure.

By the time Flynn arrives at my door I have successfully regained my sanity. We sit down at the table to have a cup of coffee before we leave. He looks very somber, he is definitely not his normal self.

"Is everything okay?" I ask.

"I've been dreading today," he tells me as he plays with the rim of his cup.

"Oh, why is that?" I ask.

Long pause.

"Because today is the day I will be giving you the last letter from Jack," he tells me.

"I see."

"I knew this day would come and that I would have to tell you that it is the last one, then I would have to watch your heart break all over again."

I can see he truly is saddened by the idea of seeing me suffer once again at the thought of losing the last thing I have to look forward to where Jack is concerned.

"Thank you," I tell him.

"Thank you? For what?" he asks, confused.

"For everything, for being there when the police came to the door, for going to get Bryna, for helping me around the house, for bringing to life this grand adventure, for giving me one last piece of Jack to hold on to," I tell him.

"And now you have to live through that loss all over

again."

"No, I don't. You have given me something that I could never have imagined. You have given me the last piece of Jack that existed in this world," I explain.

"And now there is nothing more."

"Flynn, yes of course I looked forward to each month because the hope that you would bring me a letter was there, yes I was disappointed when I didn't get one and yes it would only give me hope for the next month, but knowing that this is the last one is kind of a relief."

"How so?" he asks.

"Because I know that this is it, I don't have to wonder if there will be another, I can move on past them," I tell him.

Flynn offers a smile before he reaches into his pocket and pulls out a folded envelope. He places it on the table and slides it over to me. I take a deep breath before I tear it open.

Piper,

This will be our twenty-second Valentine's Day together. I still remember our first. I was walking through the halls of the high school with a bouquet of flowers waiting for fourth period to end. When the bell rang, I waited for you to exit your classroom and I began singing. I can't remember what song it was, I know it was horrible and off key. However, I do remember the look on your face. The shock, the horror of the public display of affection so grand that the whole school stopped to watch. Then when you saw that no one was laughing and that all the other girls wanted to be you, you finally let yourself take it in and I could see the tears of joy fill your eyes.

I had no clue that day that I would be sitting here more than twenty years later with the same beautiful girl. Don't worry. I won't be recreating anything of the sorts today, and I will not make you endure any other forms of embarrassing public displays of affection.

In high school we had no idea what each day would bring, but today we are going to take a glimpse into our future.

Keep this in mind—no matter what we are told to day, know that I will always protect you, forever be by your side and I will spend eternity loving you.

Jack

The tears did not wait until the end of the letter, they formed the moment I saw my name. Flynn sat quietly while I read and reread the letter. I am not sure at what point he grabbed the tissue box for me, but there it was ready for me to grab one to absorb the tears I cannot control.

"He loved you more than that letter could ever tell you," he tells me once I put the letter down.

"I know, and I will always love him, I just hope he knows how much. Thank you, thank you for giving him back to me, if even just for this moment."

Once my tears stop, Flynn lets me know that we were going to be seeing a Madam Kallista for a palm reading. Jack thought it would be a fun and goofy way to spend Valentine's Day.

After changing, we are soon on our way to her home to have the reading. Flynn does a good job of lightening the mood with jokes about how it is all a load of bull. Telling me that all the chick does is pick up on signals from you when all they have done is start off with a generic topic making you think they are tuned into you.

"'Cause it's real hard to tell someone that they can feel a deep pain in them when they come in with a scowl on their face, or that they see great joy when someone comes in all bubbly?" he jokes.

"I never said I believe this was real, I just always thought it would be fun and entertaining."

"I just hope you don't buy anything she is selling."

"Don't worry, I will keep an open mind."

We pull up to a house painted purple and a neon sign with a triangle and an eye in the middle of it.

"I think it is the neon light that gives them their power," I joke.

Flynn puts the car in park and we make our way to the front door. A woman fully dressed in stereotypical gypsy garb answers the door.

"Flynn, Piper, how nice of you to join me today," she greets.

"Don't read anything into that, I made an appointment," Flynn whispers.

"How did you know my name?" I ask, playing along.

"Madam Kallista knows everything, my dear. Please come in."

Madam Kallista brings us to her reading room and asks me to take a seat at the small table and offers Flynn a chair off to the side.

"Now my dear, let me have your hands," she instructs me.

Madam Kallista takes a hold of my hands, holding them palm up. She closes her eyes and concentrates on my aura. After a few moments, she opens her eyes and starts to examine my palms.

"Oh, yes you are a strong one. You have overcome many obstacles in your life."

I hear Flynn let out a small chuckle behind me.

"Haven't we all?" I ask.

"Yes, but yours are of the heart," she answers.

"I see."

"You have lost a great love. You feel this loss still today. But I see soon you will love again, she continues.

"But am I ready to love again?" I ask, playing along.

"Oh yes my dear, you already feel the weight of your loss lifting, releasing you of the guilt of taking a new lover. That release will usher in a new sense of freedom, it will allow you to love again, this is near in your future," she tells me.

"I see. Does it tell me with who?" I ask ,holding back my smile.

"The fates do not give details, they only allow me to guide you on your path," she answers.

"Hmm, I do see one more obstacle in your path to love."

Before she tells me any more, she re-examines the lines on my palm.

"You are harboring a secret, a secret that has power over you. One that only you can release."

My heart skips a beat. That has to be a standard thing to say. I mean everyone has secrets right? There is no way she could know. There is no way the lines on my palm can tell her something like that, right?

"You must let go of this power. It is darkening your heart. If you do not release this power it will grow. I see that the love awaiting you will not be able to withstand the darkness that will consume you."

What the hell. Is she for real? Is she really sitting here telling me something negative? I thought they didn't do that and only told you about the puppies and rainbows in your life.

Madam Kallista goes on to tell me some more about how I will have a long life and that it is up to me if it is lived in darkness or the light as she sees both paths, but until I make the choice my future is unclear.

"So basically, I'm at a crossroads?" I ask.

"The future is unwritten. I am here to point out the paths in front of you," she tells me.

Flynn and I thank her for her time and make our exit gracefully.

"Wow, I can't imagine why you didn't want to have your

palms read," I joke as we walk back to the car.

"I told you it was all bullshit." He laughs.

Flynn once again pulls the spade shovel from his coat pocket. We walk over to a large bush in front of the house and Flynn begins to dig a hole.

While he digs, I can't help but think about this secret that has power over me. Could she really have seen that on my palms?

Rae Matthews

Chapter Twenty-Two
Popcorn & Secrets

I call out a, "Thank you, Nancy" as I leave the hospital room.

It's been nearly a month since Flynn and I saw Madam Kallista and although I told myself I wouldn't make my visit to the hospital again after that night, I find I am still drawn to the dark, or so Madam Kallista called it. I know this is not good for me and I know I am only making it harder on myself, especially after meeting Kyle. After hearing his story and seeing the pain he has been holding on to, it was hard to leave this time.

As I open the door to my car, I tell myself this is the last time. No more. Enough is enough. I sit down in the driver's seat, staring at the large white building in front of me knowing I will be back. I'm about to turn the key to start my car when I get a text.

ABBY: Carpe Diem, your place tonight. GIRLS NIGHT
ME: Does it have to be tonight? I'm kind of tired
ABBY: Carpe Diem does NOT mean I will do it later.

ME: Fine, what time?

ABBY: Casey and I will be there at seven, movies, pizza, and pj's in tow

ME: See you then

I toss my phone on the passenger seat and head for home. Why does it have to be tonight, and why a girls night? I didn't put girls' night on my list. Is she using Carpe Diem to get me to hang out on a whim? I would not put it past her.

When I get home, I pull my list off the hutch and scan the items remaining... Then I see it.

Fun with Girlfriends

Dang it. All I want to do is order some food, then curl up with a Lifetime movie, maybe take a hot bath before bed, that is it.

Before long Abby and Casey are pounding at my door.

"Let the fun begin," Abby shouts as she makes her entrance.

"Oh goody, it's going to be tons of fun! I can just feel it," I tell her sarcastically.

"Come on, liven up. How often do we get to do this?" Casey asks.

"Um, like once a week for a while there, this is not our first ever girls night," I tell them.

"Yes we know that, but Jack didn't actually have anything planned for March. I can't blame him. It's kind of a hard month to plan for given the items left on your list... so here we are," Abby tells me.

"I see. Well, we could have just skipped this month then." I laugh.

"Nope, skipping a month was not part of the plan," Abby blurts.

"So this is the best you guys and Flynn could come up with? You could have created a new item," I tell her.

"Don't get her started, she wanted us to go to one of those pole dancing classes," Casey tells me.

I look to Abby and see the grin on her face indicating that if it were up to Abby alone, I would probably be swinging from a pole right now.

"Movies it is," I agree.

Three slices of pizza, two bottles of wine, and a chick flick later, we are on to the gossip portion of the evening.

Abby is busy ranting on about this new receptionist at Dave's office, and how she is always dressed in short, inappropriate skirts with tiny tops. She is pissed at how no one seems to care.

"Hello, dress codes are there for a reason people, they need to be enforced."

"I hear ya," I agree.

"So did Flynn tell you about the girl he has been seeing?"

She *just* had to wait until I was taking a sip of wine to drop that bomb. I spray my wine all over the coffee table when I hear the news.

"Huh? No, he didn't."

"I guess he has only seen her a few times. Her name is Keriann," she tells me.

"So he told you about her?" I ask, trying to keep my cool.

"No, actually Dave and I ran into them the other night at the movie theater."

"I see. Is she nice?" I ask.

I don't pay attention to the answer, my mind is fluttering. Why didn't he tell me? I've talked or texted with him almost every day for the last two years? Why wouldn't he tell me something like this? Is he keeping her a secret? Is she a bitch? I bet she is a bitch or psycho. I bet she is psycho. I know I am reaching for a reason to hate her before I meet her, deep down I know that she is probably perfect. Flynn does not waste time with women he doesn't see a possible future with. If he picks up on any signs that they are drama queens, high maintenance, or self-centeredness in any of them, he drops them faster than a hot potato.

"Are you listening?" Casey asks.

"Yeah, sure, she's ugly?" I say without thinking.

"She didn't say she was ugly?" Casey tells me.

"No, I didn't mean ugly. I... um... no, I wasn't listening," I confess.

"Are you jealous?" Abby asks with a smile.

How do I answer that? My mind reminds me I have no reason to be jealous. However, my body has other ideas, my heart is beating like a drum, my armpits are starting to sweat, and my palms are getting clammy. All the signs point to yes. on the other hand, I have absolutely no right to be jealous.

"No, why would I be jealous?" I ask.

"I don't know, you tell me."

"No, I think I'm surprised he hadn't said anything to me. I talked to him yesterday and we texted this morning," I tell her.

"Uh-huh, that must be it."

I quickly change the subject. My body starts to calm, but my brain did not get the memo. I can't stop thinking about Flynn. I know I convinced myself that the feelings I had after the ski hill were fake, but now I'm starting to wondering again if that is true. However, even if my feelings are true, it is obvious whatever I saw in his eyes that day was all part of my imagination. If he felt anything for me he wouldn't be out dating.

"So how was the physic, you never told me," Casey asks, bringing my thoughts back.

"Oh you know, the same old crap you hear about from anyone who has a reading," I tell her.

"So what did she say," she asks again.

"That I would love again soon but my path to love is unclear or some crap," I tell her.

"What the heck does that mean," she asks.

"I don't know."

"She say anything else?"

I pause before I answer. This could be my chance to expose my secret. If I tell them, they can help me fight the urge. They can be a louder voice of reason. What will they think? Will they have me committed? Will they embrace the crazy? Screw it.

"She did say something about a secret and that it has too much power over me," I tell them.

"Ha, secret. Now you know she is full of it, you tell us everything." Abby laughs.

"Well... not everything." I hesitate.

Abby and Casey look at each other in shock. I'm sure it hurt to hear that I have a secret with that much power that I haven't told them about. Up until now, we had told each other everything, everything big anyway. There were no secrets between us. Especially not one some quack psychic could make me think twice about.

"So a few months after Jack died, I started doing something that I know is not good for me," I start.

"Shit! You're doing drugs. I knew you had to be on something," Casey shouts.

"No, it's not drugs," I confirm.

"Then what?"

"I have been going to the hospital." I cringe as I say the words.

"I don't get it?" Abby says.

Casey's eyes go from confusion to shock once she realizes what I'm telling them.

"You're not?" she begged.

"I know, it's not good."

"I don't get it," Abby calls out.

"She is visiting the fifth floor," Casey tells her.

"What is on the fifth floor?" Abby asks in frustration.

Casey and I sit back and stare at her. Waiting for her to

put two and two together because neither of us wants to actually say the words.

It takes her longer than I thought before the light bulb finally comes on.

"Nooooooo. Piper! What are you thinking?"

Chapter Twenty-Three

April Showers Brings May Flowers

It's April, the month I will never be able to enjoy again. The month that Jack was taken from me. I can already feel the change in my attitude. Bryna's even walking on eggshells when she talks to me. Everyone is better than last year so I suppose I am thankful for that. And I suppose that over time everyone will be able treat this month like any other.

Abby has been stopping by more and more even though I have explained to her repeatedly that I am fine, although I shouldn't complain. I love that they all care so much and know this month is hard to live through.

To be honest, I would have expected this month to be much worse than it is starting out to be. I would have expected myself to want to crawl into a hole and never come out similar to last year.

However, this last year has been amazing, it has had its moments, as all years do. Waking up each day has gotten easier and easier. The days have been filled with more than feeling sorry for myself or grief for Jack. Each day is filled with hope. Hope that soon I will be on my way to crossing off another item on my list. Hope that I will seize each day *even* if that means whatever is happening was not on my list. Hope that once my list is done, I will not stop there, I will keep adding to it.

The last few weeks have been weird so my hope has dwindled some. Flynn is dating some chick that he still hasn't told me about. I have given him plenty of opportunities to let the cat out of the bag, nothing. I get nothing. A brush off or he completely ignores the question. I am running out of polite ways to bring it up, next will be a blurted, accusing type question.

My only distraction to that is that Casey and Abby have been on me like stink on a skunk to make sure I stop my now-not-so secret visits to the hospital.

I thought I would regret telling them about my visits to the fifth floor. I am so glad I don't. They have been a huge help. I haven't been back since. Yes, it has only been a few weeks and I have gone weeks without going before. This time, it feels different. I don't yet feel that pull tugging at me.

The weather change has been a long time coming and could be another reason why my urges have been curbed. I love spring. Everything is coming to life, the fresh smell of the rain coming through the open windows. Last year I barely acknowledged the robins picking at the worms in my yard. Today I have been standing at the kitchen window for what seems like forever watching the life return.

The birds are chirping and excited to be back, the grass is starting to turn green, the trees are budding and will soon be covered in leaves once again. I could have sat here for the rest of the day with my thoughts had my phone not buzzed.

FLYNN: What are you doing tonight?
ME: No plans... I take it I have some now?
FLYNN: Dinner at my place?
ME: Sure, what time?

FLYNN: How does seven sound?
ME: Sounds good... Carpe Diem?
FLYNN: You got it!

Flynn, still carrying out Jack's plan after all these months. Not that I thought he would give up or lose interest, I thought maybe he would get it started and pass it off to Casey or Abby once things got underway. I love that he has taken such care in making sure each adventure is cared for and planned out as Jack would have wanted. Even after all these months, I still find it hard to think of all the years Jack put into planning this. All those years of him planning and saving and bragging to Flynn, then he is taken before he can see the look on my face when his plan is revealed.

Deep down I always knew that Flynn was a good friend to Jack. They have been through so much together. I love Flynn for being such a great friend to Jack and now to me.

My thoughts have run away with me again and before I know it it's time to get ready for dinner. I shower and pick out a nice spring dress to wear. I am not normally a dress person, however, the spring air is begging for a dress tonight.

An hour later, I am walking out the door. The warm air caresses my skin and I can't help but smile. I have no idea what tonight will bring, but I can't wait.

Flynn is pretty vague about what tonight is supposed to be, despite all my attempts to get it out of him. So far, we enjoyed a wonderful lasagna dinner. Flynn joked that it was about all he could make without burning the hell out of it. We have had great conversations about everything under the sun. The only think I haven't been able to get him to talk about is Keriann. I may have to blurt it out or allow my head to explode. Why won't he tell me about her? What is with all the secrecy?

Flynn put on some soft music and we move outside to the front porch to continue our conversation. The air has cooled. I look up at the night sky, not a star to be seen, the moisture in the air is building giving out an unmistakable scent.

"Smells like rain," I say.

"I love that smell," Flynn replies.

"So do I. It is always so refreshing."

His eyes are glued to mine, a smile on his face that is pure happiness. I haven't seen him like this since... actually come to think of it, I'm not sure I have ever seen him look this content.

Flynn gets up suddenly and goes back into the house. He isn't gone very long, the light that was radiating through the window is gone and is replaced by a flickering glow. When Flynn returns, he has several small candles, a bottle of wine and two glasses in his arms. I help him juggle them and watch as he lights each candle and sets them around us.

"I hope you don't mind, I enjoy a glass of wine and some candles when I get ready to enjoy a spring storm," Flynn tells me.

I have to fight back the laughter. I can't tell if he is for real or messing with me.

"Really?" I ask.

"I do. Not all the time, but when I sit out here to enjoy them I do," he tells me.

"So is that when you turn in your man card and make a trip to Hobby Lobby to buy potpourri?" I joke.

"Haha laugh it up, chuckles..."

"I'm sorry, you caught me off guard. I guess I've never seen this side of you before."

"It's not one I advertise."

"You should. You would have the ladies crawling all over you."

As soon as the words come out of my mouth, my heart starts to beat faster and my stomach starts to turn. Just the thought of ladies, crawling all over him makes me sick.

Why? Why would I care? Maybe this is because I know he is keeping his current lady a secret. He has to know Abby would have mentioned it.

Flynn never responded to my little joke, he is watching his glass as he swirls the wine. Maybe he and Keriann are more serious than I knew.

"Okay, I have to ask. I've been trying to keep my nose out of it, but I'm a woman, I can't, it's against my nature... Why haven't you mentioned that you are dating someone?" I calmly ask.

His eye shot up to mine. Surprise? Confusion? I'm not sure about the look in his eyes.

"I'm not dating anyone," he says.

"Really, because Abby said you were dating someone named Keriann," I tell him.

"Keriann is an acquaintance that was helping me out with something," he explains.

"Oh, Abby seemed to be under the impression that you had been dating for a little while."

"No, she misunderstood."

I feel a weight lift from my chest. Relief that he wasn't hiding anything or anyone from me? Yes, that is what I'm going with.

The rain starts to fall interrupting the awkward silence that is hanging in the air. I close my eyes and take a deep breath. The wine, the glow of the candles, and now the smell of the rain is intoxicating.

When I open my eyes, I see Flynn once again looking at his wine glass, this time he is caressing the edge with his thumb. He looks nervous.

"So are you going to finally tell me what tonight is all about?" I ask softly.

He gives a small smile before setting his glass down on the table between us. He stands and moves in front of me. Slowly he reaches for my glass and sets it on the table. Then reaching for my hand, he helps me to my feet. I do not say a word as I follow his lead.

To my surprise he walks me to the steps leading down from the porch and has me wait there while he walks back inside the house, I hear the music that was once soft now projecting out to the front yard. The song is "Chandelier" by Sia, a song I love. When Flynn returns, he grabs my hand once more and guides me down the stairs to the front lawn.

"What are we doing?" I laugh as the rain kisses my skin.

"We are going to dance in the rain," he tells me with a large smile on his face.

"Come on, no way," I say with surprise.

Flynn claps his hands loudly and the trees and bushes come to light with white lights.

"Oh, you're good," I inform him.

"I know." He gloats proudly.

"No really, this would have any woman melting in your arms," I tell him.

He continues to smile as he grabs my hand, places his arm around my waist, and begins moving us to the rhythm of the song.

He leads me like a pro, and the world fades away. It's as if Flynn and I are the only ones who exist. Our eyes are locked, neither of us seems to want to look away. A strange feeling is rushing over me, one I have felt before. One I should not be feeling. Distraction. I need a distraction.

"I didn't know you could dance like this."

"Neither did I."

"Flynn, you are forty-one, how could you not know you could dance like this?"

"Because my dance teacher, Keriann, has been teaching me for the last six weeks. But, in the end, I wasn't sure I could pull it off," he explains.

As he finishes he pushes me out, keeping a firm grip on my hand. He pulls me back guiding me into a spin. Our bodies move in one fluid motion. That is until the big finish. Flynn attempts to end the song with a dip. However, his foot slips and we end up in a puddle of water, laughing wildly.

Flynn helps me up when I hear a new song start to play. It has a familiar beat, but I can't place it. I know I like it, I know I have heard it a million times before. Still lying on the ground, I start to move to the intoxicating beat. I am still lost as to the name of the song, until the first line.

I jump to my feet and start stomping my feet as "Are you Going To Be My Girl" by Jet plays. Flynn soon joins in with my crazy dancing. We slip and slide, splashing the water that has formed in the divots of the yard.

Chapter Twenty-Four
The Last Word

Our crazy dance marathon continues for a few more songs. Things slow back down when the song everyone knows from one of the most iconic movie scenes ever.

My thoughts go to the white, single-shoulder dress, white satin shoes, and a line full of firefighters waiting for their turn to dance with an angel. Of course, I am thinking about the movie *Always*. The movie where Richard Dreyfuss plays the ghost of Holly Hunter's lost love.

Flynn moves closer to me, he brings his body next to mine and begins to guide our movements. Soon I find my head resting on his shoulder. I have given complete control over to him. The warmth of his body next to mine is exhilarating. I can feel his heart beating rapidly in sync with mine.

The details are unclear as to how. All I know is that the next thing I know, our lips are locked. His lips are so soft. His touch is gentle. Flynn scoops me up into his arms and carries me into the house. The screen door slams behind us as he continues on to his bedroom.

Flynn places me softly onto the bed. He removes his wet shirt and leans down to me. We quickly pick up where we left off outside. I wrap my legs around him. His hand lands on my calf and moves up my thigh. He is kissing my neck and I can feel my excitement growing. Then the weight of what I want to happen hits me when I feel Flynn slip his hand further up my dress.

"Stop!" I call out.

"I'm sorry... Did I hurt you?"

"No, you are perfect, I just... I can't," I tell him.

"Did I do something wrong?" he asks softly.

"No, it's not you, I..." I trail off.

"You don't have to explain."

Flynn gets up from the bed and moves toward his closet. A moment later, he comes back to me and lays a shirt and some sweatpants at the end of the bed.

"Here, you're going to want to get out of those wet clothes," he says, offering a smile.

"Flynn... I'm so sorry, I..."

"No, you never need to be sorry with me. I completely understand," he tells me as he sits on the edge of the bed. "If you had done something today that you were not comfortable with then I would never have forgiven myself," he continues.

"Thank you... but I..."

"No buts, Piper. I would never in a million years want this if you didn't."

"I think I was overcome by the evening. It was so special and perfect."

"Piper, you don't need to explain. I will go to the other room to change and I will meet you on the porch, take your time."

Flynn kisses my forehead, grabs a second set of clothing, and closes his bedroom door as he leaves.

I take my time changing, partly because I need a few moments to myself to gather my thoughts and partly because

I am embarrassed as all hell that I almost made a huge mistake.

Tonight has been perfect—dinner, the wine, and dancing. Flynn obviously put a lot of effort into tonight. The dance lessons and the white lights covering his large tree and bushes.

I smile as the memories of the evening come flooding back. The moment I realized that Flynn was not holding back on a girl he was supposedly seeing. Leave it to Abby to get the details wrong.

My heart starts to race again when I think of the kiss we shared not long ago in the rain. The passion in that kiss was magical. I haven't felt that magic in almost two years. My face is warm with a blush as I think about what could have been this evening.

"Stop it!" I yell to myself.

I open the door to the bedroom and make my way to the bathroom to splash some water on my face. The last thing I need is for Flynn to see me like that. I've embarrassed myself enough for one night.

After fixing myself up I start to head outside to meet Flynn, I walk by my purse. A thought comes to me. I look toward the front window; Flynn is sitting with his back to the window, sipping on his glass of wine.

Perfect. I reach into my purse and retrieve the red shard. I stand staring at it in my hand for a moment before I make my way back to Flynn's room.

I walk over to his nightstand and place it next to his alarm clock. I think this is the right spot for this one. As I turn to leave, I notice the writing on a piece of paper next to the lamp. I see Jack's handwriting that says, "Flynn." A letter from Jack to Flynn?

I don't know what made me pick it up. It is a complete invasion of privacy that I would have thought unforgivable. To read someone's last words to someone, that is not you. Unfortunately for my voice of reason, I have not been thinking clearly all night. I open the worn paper and read.

Flynn,

I guess this is it, the big good-bye. I don't have much to say to you that I haven't already said in life, so I will just say this.

You have been my friend for as long as I can remember, but you have been more like a brother to me. Your friendship and support over the years has meant the world to me. I could not have asked for or found a better man to call my friend.

If I can ask you one last favor. Look after our girl. Be there for her, comfort her, clean the gutters for her. Also, watch over Bryna and if I die before she is married make sure she doesn't end up with some jackass, and should that day come, if she asks you, know that you have my blessing to give her away.

I wouldn't trust them in the care of anyone other than you. Be well my friend and take care.

Jack

P.S. Also, if I die younger than I would like and you are still single, I want to tell you that if you should find your happiness, know that you have my wholehearted blessing. I would not trust anyone else with her heart.

Jack's words wash over me and I feel the tears starting to fight their way out.

"What are you doing?"

His words startle me. And I drop the letter on the floor. The look on Flynn's face of anger, hurt and shock all rolled into one.

"I'm sorry, I shouldn't have," I confess.

"No, you shouldn't have," he says, walking toward me.

Regret immediately rushed over my body. I knew it was wrong. If I had asked him if I could read it, he might have said yes, but now I have betrayed his privacy and I will never know if he would have shared this with me.

I lean down and pick up the letter, fold it, and hand it to Flynn.

"This was meant for me."

"I know, I'm sorry. I was leaving you a gift, and then I saw it laying there. I don't know what came over me."

Flynn doesn't say anything as he places the letter in the drawer of his nightstand and then leaves the room.

I follow Flynn, apologizing repeatedly. He accepts my apology halfheartedly and begins tossing dishes into the sink.

"Maybe I should go," I offer.

"I think that would be a good idea."

Rae Matthews

Chapter Twenty-Five

Forgiveness

That brings us to today... Today is the second anniversary of Jack's death. We all made plans to meet for dinner and then visit Jack.

I have not spoken to Flynn since that night. I have tried to call, text him, but he doesn't answer or respond. I confessed to Abby and Casey everything that happened that night and what I had done. They both agree he just needs some time to cool off, he could never cut Bryna and me out of his life. One could say he is being stubborn about this. I, however, can't blame him, I would have felt the same way. Since I am the one at fault, I need to be willing to give him the time he needs to forgive my actions.

Although there was nothing in the letter that I felt was overly personal, I can understand that it was still a huge invasion of privacy. All I can do is hope that today he will break his silent treatment.

These last nine months since I was given this most unexpected gift have been amazing and I would hate for my one mistake to put a dark cloud over everything Flynn has done for me in Jack's honor.

Sitting here applying my makeup in an effort to get ready for dinner, it doesn't feel real that Jack has been gone two years already.

I can't stop thinking about the last nine months. The gift Jack has been so thoughtful in creating and so well planned that even though he was meant to be here with me on this grand adventure, and though he couldn't be, I still felt him here with me helping me. This grand plan that was meant to be a surprise anniversary gift has turned into the best possible way he could have said good-bye to me.

After getting dressed, I have just one last thing to do before dinner. It may not have been on the agenda for today, but, I think it is what I need to do. It feels right and I think it is time. After all, how can I ask others to forgive me when I hold on to so much anger? Looking at the clock, I verify I have plenty of time before I have to meet everyone at the restaurant.

Fifteen minutes later, I am walking through the halls of the fifth floor, the coma ward of the hospital. I have walked these halls more times than I care to admit, but I know in my heart this will be the last time. It's bittersweet really, I used to come here to channel help my anger and help my grief. It was a comfort and a curse at the same time.

The curse was walking down this hall to Helen's room, knowing that the woman responsible for taking Jack from me was right in front of me, having her close enough to touch, but knowing that no matter what, me being this close will never mean anything to her, because she was in a coma. That knowledge was a hell of my own making.

I thought I needed some justice, an apology, some whatever you want to call it to be happy again. There were days I would wish she would wake up so I could make her feel the pain she caused me, other times I found comfort in the thought that the limbo she was in, being neither dead nor alive was hell for her, but those were not my thoughts today.

Today I feel peace. I feel like things will happen in this world and no one can predict or prevent the things fate has planned for us. Today I say my good-bye to Helen, and to all that anger. Today I forgive her.

As I approach her room Nancy Jacobs the day nurse grabs at my attention, she is on the phone, but the look in her eyes with her frantic motions causes me to stop at the nurses' desk. She takes a breath and holds out her hand and motions for me to wait until she is off the phone.

"Okay, yes thank you, yes, I have to go. Thank you…" Nancy says while hanging up the phone.

"What's going on?" I ask.

"Honey, I'm so glad I caught you, you can't go in there," she says, trying to hide her panic.

"Why, what happened, did she die?" I ask, not knowing how the answer would make me feel if the answer was yes.

"No, she didn't die. I *really* can't talk about it with you, since you are not family…" she says, trailing off at the end.

She has never said that to me before. She has always found a way to let me know what the status of her condition is.

"Nancy, I understand that. However, today was to be my final visit, I had hoped to say my peace and be gone. I know you have bent the rules for me to visit her the last two years, but can you make one more exception? I promise I will be quick, no one will know I was here," I plead.

"Mrs. Reynolds, I seriously can't. And all I can tell you is that she did not *die.*"

She whispers the word die and gives me a strange look as if I am supposed to pick up on this new code. I look at her in confusion, still not understanding the meaning, and then BAM, it hits me like a ton of bricks.

"SHE WOKE UP?" I yell.

"I'm sorry I cannot release patient statuses to anyone but family," she says while she nods her head yes.

"I have to see her," I scream.

My mind is filled with a haze. The woman who took Jack from us has woken up. All those days of sitting at her bedside, staring at her, wishing I could explain to her exactly what she took from me. All those days of being happy that she was stuck in limbo.

Nancy can't get around the nursing desk fast enough to stop me. I dart toward room 508, the room I have spent so many hours in. I place my hand on the knob and turn with no thought to what I will say when I get on the other side.

Kyle is startled when he sees it is me coming through the door. Helen has a look of confusion, why would she know me? She has been in a coma since that day. She slept for the last two years, peacefully unaware of what she took from me.

"Mrs. Reynolds, you can't be in here!" Nancy yells, pulling at my arm.

"It's okay, Nancy, thank you," Helen says to my surprise.

"Are you sure?" Nancy asks before releasing my arm.

"Yes, thank you."

I'm speechless. All the things I planned to say to a comatose Helen are gone from my mind. Never in a million years would I have thought she would ever wake up. Nancy informed me long ago that it didn't look good and that they were basically waiting for her body to give up.

"Hello, Piper is it?" Helen says.

I look to Kyle before I confirm

"I already told her everything," Kyle tells me.

"Yes, I'm Piper," I say, forcing the words.

"Piper, I cannot tell you how sorry I am," Helen tells me.

"I, I came here to…" I can't finish my thought

"It's okay, Piper, whatever you need to say to me I deserve it," Helen tells me.

Kyle and Helen both stare at me waiting for me to speak. After a few moments, my heart starts to slow and I can breathe easier.

"How, how are you awake?" I ask.

"The doctors don't know for sure, they are still waiting for some tests, but for now, they think her brain healed itself," Kyle informs me.

"And how long have you been awake?"

"About a week," she tells me.

"I see, and Kyle told you about Jack?"

"Yes, he did. Piper, I know that there is nothing I can say to bring your husband back, but please know how sorry I am. If I could take his place, I would."

The words hang in the air. If she could take his place, she would. Nevertheless, she can't. Jack is gone and now she lies here, awake, on her way to what appears to be a full recovery.

My anger starts to rear its ugly head and then I smell it. Coffee. I look around the room, not a coffee cup to be found, I open the door and look into the hallway. Nancy is standing at the nurses' station. She looks and gives me an inquisitive look. I look around and see no one else. I close the door and turn my attention back to Helen and Kyle. It is then that a strange sensation comes over me. It is a calm that I have not felt in a long time, a calm that reminds me of why I am here today.

"Today is the two year anniversary, did you know that?" I ask.

"Yes, I know…" Helen starts.

"No please," I interrupt.

"Okay."

"Did you know that I used to visit you?"

"No, I didn't."

"I used to sit by your bedside and tell you about all the things I thought I wanted to say to your face. I would tell you how you deserved to die for what you took from me."

"Piper…"

"No, let me finish."

"All right."

"I used to tell you about all the things Jack was missing

out on, how much I missed him, and how much I hated you. I would dream about a day that I would get to say all those hurtful things to you."

I can see the tears forming in her eyes. Mine are falling down my cheeks.

"But today I came to offer my forgiveness."

Kyle's head springs up. He had been staring at the floor avoiding eye contact while I had my little speech. Helen's tears are flowing faster than mine.

"I admit, I was shocked when I found you awake as I thought I was going to be talking to the same Helen I had for the last two years. But that shouldn't change why I am here. I am glad to be able to say this to you as you are now."

"Piper, I don't deserve your forgiveness. I took your husband from you and that is unforgivable." Helen sobs.

"You have it nonetheless. I forgive you. You did not set out to take my husband from me, you made a mistake. You have paid for it with two years of your life taken from you."

"Piper I... I..." Helen tries to speak, but the tears hold back her words.

"I will leave you to it, I won't be back. I need to move on from this and I can't do that if I am holding on to such anger toward you." I say, reaching for the door handle.

"I don't know what to say," Kyle says.

"Nothing needs to be said. All I ask is that you live the best life you can and seize each day as if it could be your last," I say and then exit the room.

Chapter Twenty-Six
Full Circle

The walk to the car seems to take only a few seconds. I do not remember walking down the hall, getting on the elevator, or exiting the hospital. My thoughts were consumed with Jack.

I know in my heart that Jack was with me moments ago giving me the strength to do what was right. I know that he was standing next to me giving me the courage to forgive. As soon as I left the room, I felt he was gone. As if he had been with me, watching over me, waiting to be there for me this one last time.

I hesitate to put the key in the ignition, I need a minute or two to sit and do nothing. I pay no attention to any one thing as I look around the parking lot. People are coming and going from the hospital. Today is the last day I would be one of these people. I look over to the right and see there is a tree not far from my car that looks like a tree Jack would have liked. I reach slowly into my purse search for the small red piece of mug I had originally planned to leave with Helen.

I jump out of my car and walk over to the tree. At the

base, I use my hands to dig a small hole and place the shard into it before I refill it. A smile comes to my face and I know that I have done the right thing today, for me and for Jack. My dark secret is done and will not cloud my path to being happy.

The cool raindrops hitting my skin startles me. I didn't realize it was supposed to rain today. I look to the sky and see the dark clouds moving in. The rain starts pouring as soon as I get back into my car.

Taking one last look around, knowing this would be my last visit, I slowly pull out of the parking spot and head toward the restaurant. The rain is coming down harder, the first big storm of the year. The lighting flashing so brightly would make this a perfect day to sit at home with a glass of wine ready to watch the show.

I hear my phone buzzing in my purse. I'm sure it is Abby making sure I am on my way. I don't dare look with the rain making it hard to see more than ten feet in front of you.

I look down at the clock when a bright flash of light blinds me. I hear what sounds like a small explosion and when my eyes are back on the road I barely have enough time to swerve to the left, barely avoiding the large tree limb falling in front of me.

I can hear the small branches scratching against the metal of my car. It sounds like a banshee screaming. When I pass the tree, I swerve back into my lane. The cement is drenched with a mixture of the rain and oils from cars making it hard to gain control. I quickly move my steering wheel to correct the tailspins.

When I have full control of my car, again I take a look in my rearview mirror to get a look at the fallen limb. It nearly fills the road, how I managed to slip through is a miracle. My heart is beating rapidly as I take deep breaths to try to calm myself. When my hands start to shake, I decide to pull over to the side of the road to shake it off.

"Holy shit that was close," I tell myself.

With my hands still shaking, I dig my cell phone out of my purse to see who was calling. I slowly punch in the security code and see that I have three missed calls from Abby, five from Casey, two from Bryna and two missed calls from Flynn. They all left voice mails.

A nervous smile forms when I decide to start with Flynn's message.

"Piper, where are you? Abby and Casey said you are not at home or the restaurant or answering your phone, there is a severe storm warning, we are canceling dinner. You need to call me. I'm worried about you, please call me."

So note to future self, in order to get Flynn to talk to you after you fuck up I just need to go MIA for a short time. I didn't mean to worry anyone, they must have been calling while I was sitting by the tree. I do not understand why everyone is so worried, it's not like I have never survived a storm before.

I am about to dial Flynn when headlights catch my eye. They are wild and coming right at me like a freight train.

"Oh my God, no," I scream.

Rae Matthews

Chapter Twenty-Seven
Not Again
~ *Flynn* ~

Why the hell isn't she answering her damn phone? I know I haven't been the greatest friend the last few weeks, I've been ignoring her calls, avoiding her text messages like a pouting teenager who found out his mom went through his room. I should not have reacted the way I did, I should have allowed her to apologize and then moved on. I know she would never do anything to hurt me, we have been friends far too long and gone through too much to let this stupidity get in the way of that.

I've been thinking over the last few weeks as to why I am so pissed about her reading Jack's letter. I had every intention of showing it to her one day, so should it matter she found it and was so overcome that she read it before I was ready?

Hell, before she put on the brakes we were about to cross a line we could never cross back from. Part of me wonders what would have happened if she had not stopped us. Would she have felt it was a mistake or would it have been everything I... My thoughts are interrupted by the ringing of my phone. The caller ID holds a number I do not recognize.

"Hello," I say, answering the call.

"Hello, is this Mister Flynn Avery?"

"Yes, who is this?" I ask.

"Hello, sir. This is Peggy Williams at Hartland Community Hospital. Do you know a Piper Reynolds?" she asks.

"Yes, what's going on?"

"Sir, Mrs. Reynolds has been involved in a motor vehicle accident."

"Is she alright?" My heart skips a beat as the question leaves me.

"Sir, she is in critical condition. How soon can you get here?"

The phone nearly falls from my hand. How can this be happening? This cannot be happening.

"Sir, are you there?" Peggy asks.

"Yes, I am here."

"Sir, Piper has you listed as her emergency contact and medical power of attorney. When would you be able to get here?"

"I am on my way," I tell her.

This cannot be happening, not to Piper. She has been through so much. She doesn't deserve this.

After calling Casey to tell her, she, of course, is in a panic. Abby, Bryna, and she have been waiting at the house for Piper to surface. I grab my keys and I'm on my way to the hospital.

The drive to the hospital is surreal. Concentrating on driving through the raging storm is the only thing keeping my thoughts from taking over. When I pull into the parking lot I don't bother to reach for my umbrella, I run as quickly as I can to the emergency room door.

"I'm looking for Piper Reynolds," I tell the nurse sitting at the desk in front of me.

She punches the keys on her keyboard quickly to find the

information. She sees the desperation in my eyes.

"Yes, the doctor is waiting for you. If you can take a seat for a moment, I will let her know you are here," she tells me.

I nod in acknowledgment but do not bother to sit. I start pacing the small waiting area, my clothing dripping a trail behind me. I do not wait long for the doctor.

"Mr. Avery?" a woman in a doctor's coat asks, walking toward me.

"Yes, how is she, when can I see her?" I ask.

"Sir, my name is Doctor Redding. I am a trauma surgeon working on Piper's case. Piper sustained a heavy head injury along with some abdominal trauma as a result of the crash. I have ordered a CAT scan and MRI to gauge the extent of her injuries and should have those results any time now. Right now I can tell you that we did have to intubate her and that she is not conscious and that we are doing everything we can for her," she explains.

"When can I see her?" I ask her again.

"I can allow you to see her for only a few minutes right now, but as I said she is not conscious," she tells me.

"I don't care, I want to see her."

Doctor Redding brings me to a room filled with machines, all of them attached to Piper. I cannot control the tears falling from my eyes when I see her.

"I will give you a few minutes," she tells me before leaving me.

The beeping of the cords running from Piper to the machines monitoring her heart, the tube coming out of her beautiful mouth helping her breathe, the blood painted on her angelic face, is the hardest thing I have ever had to see.

I walk over and take her hand in mine. She doesn't respond. My thumb caresses her silky skin, again no response. I lean down to her ear in the hope that she can hear me.

"Piper, don't you dare leave me. I cannot tolerate watching you die before you know the truth," I whisper.

No response.

"Piper, you fight this, you come back to us. Come back to me," I continue.

A nurse comes in and tells me that my time is up and that there is a woman in the waiting room asking for me. I kiss Piper's forehead, wipe my tears, and follow her out.

When I enter the waiting room, everyone is there—Bryna, Casey, Chuck, Abby, and Dave.

"How is my mom?" Bryna asks, running to me with tears streaming down her face.

"They don't know yet. They should have some information for us soon. All they know for sure right now is that she did have a head injury and some abdominal trauma," I tell them.

"Can we see her?" she asks.

"Bryna, you don't want to see her right now," I tell her.

She can see why in my eyes. I pull her into my arms and hold her tight. Her sobs grow stronger the tighter I hold her. I look to Casey and Abby who are currently looking to their husbands for comfort but like me, they are having a hard time holding back the tears themselves.

About twenty minutes into our silent vigil, Doctor Redding approaches us.

"How bad is it?" I ask.

"After reviewing the test results, the good news is the head injury is not as severe as we feared. She does have some swelling but it should subside on its own," she states.

I hear a gasp of relief from behind me.

"And what is the bad news?" I ask.

"She is going into liver failure. We have her stabilized for now. We also see a large mass on her liver in the scan. Between the injuries and the mass she will need a liver transplant," she tells us.

"Is it cancer?" I ask.

"We can't be certain without taking a biopsy."

"Okay, so we get her a new liver," Bryna shouts.

"I'm afraid it is not that simple. Piper is O positive, making finding a compatible liver harder. We are already taking steps to get her on the transplant list, but we may not find one in time."

"Take part of mine, you can do that right? Use a living donor?" Abby says, rushing to my side.

"Yes, we can. The donor needs to meet some basic criteria then we can run type matching to see if you would be an ideal donor," Doctor Redding explains.

"First do you or anyone willing to be tested have an O positive or O negative blood type?" she asks.

Silence, everyone looks beaten down and losing hope by each passing second.

"Bryna?" someone finally asks.

"No, I'm B. Dad was AB," she tells us.

"Then I'm sorry. There is no way we can proceed with the type matching," Doctor Redding tells us.

"I do," a familiar voice calls out.

My head whips around to see Kyle standing in the hall right outside the door.

"What in the hell are you doing here?" I demand, walking toward him.

"I heard Piper was hurt. I came down to see if she was okay. I want to help if I can."

"You and your wife have done enough," I yell.

"FLYNN! STOP IT," Bryna yells.

"I don't know what is going on, but if he wants to help my mom then let him," she continues sternly.

She is her mother's daughter, able to command attention and bring about the voice of reason in all of us. I know she is right and that my dislike for Kyle or his wife should not get in the way of saving Piper.

"You're right, I'm sorry."

Chapter Twenty-Eight

Thankful

~ Flynn ~

It has been a month since we got the news that Kyle was not a match. The devastation almost killed me. That is until Helen offered to be tested. She was O positive and willing to do whatever she could for Piper. The doctors originally advised against it, cautioning her against the risks.

Helen didn't care and insisted on being tested. In a twist of fate, she was the best match possible. The doctors insisted on waiting to perform the transplant until Helen had regained some strength since Piper was stable, today is that day.

Piper has been stable, but still unconscious in a medically induced coma. I have been by her side each and every day waiting for this day. The doctors felt keeping her in the coma would give her brain a better chance to heal.

Bryna has been here with me, we would take turns talking to her and giving each other support. She has been so brave, first losing her father and now her mother lays before us with her future uncertain.

"It's time," Doctor Redding tells us.

"Okay, thank you," I reply.

I lean down to kiss Piper's hand as I have done each day. I move to whisper in her ear.

"You are going to survive this, you are going to come back to us, come back to me, so that I can tell you how much I love you."

I wipe the tear falling from my eye before standing and moving to allow Bryna to say what she needs to say.

To give her some privacy, I move to the other side of the room. I see the tears falling from her eyes as she whispers into her mother's ear. I want to promise her that everything will be okay, but I can't.

We watch as the nurses' wheel the bed out to the hall and down to the operating room. A moment later, we see Helen being wheeled down the hall also.

"Helen," I yell, running to her side.

"Flynn…"

"I want to thank you. I know you didn't have to do this, that it is a risk. I just want you to know that whatever happens…" I am unable to finish.

"Flynn, if this is all I can do to somehow right the wrong I caused then I will do it, no matter my fate, it is the right thing to do," she tells me before signaling the nurse to continue on.

The next few hours pass as if they are days. The doctor told us it could be four to eight hours for the surgery.

Hour One

Abby and Casey try to convince Bryna to lie down and get some rest but she refuses. They tried with me briefly, but could see that even though I did not sleep much last night, there was no way I was going to rest now. I cannot rest until I know Piper is okay.

With nothing else to do but think, my mind wanders to the first day I met Piper.

It was Christmas break, Jack and his family had taken a family vacation to visit some family so I was stuck without my best friend for winter break.

Since our yearly ritual of wintertime shenanigans was off and with my mom insisting I not mope around the house I spent most of my time at the movies or at the arcade. It was when I went to go see *Star Trek VI: The Undiscovered Country* for the third time.

I had just gotten my pop, popcorn, and candy and was on my way to the theater number three when a girl came running around the corner knocking everything out of my hand. I had never seen a girl so beautiful. The way her cheeks flushed with embarrassment only added to her beauty. She immediately started apologizing and offered to buy me a new popcorn and pop. I, of course, took all the blame and told her she didn't have to.

When she asked what movie I was there to see, I stuttered trying to get the words to form but finally managed to tell her Star Trek. She told me she and her sister were also there to see Star Trek and would be happy to share their popcorn. I happily accepted. She told me to wait where I was while she used the bathroom and then would take me to their seats. Afterward, we went out for pizza so she could once again apologize for spilling my popcorn.

She told me all about how they had just moved to town and would be starting school here after the break, I couldn't help but wonder if we would have any classes together. When we were finished, she gave me her phone number and told me to give her a call sometime. This was the first time a girl had ever given me her phone number. I was in shock that someone like her would want to give someone like me her phone number, so like an idiot, I didn't call her right away.

A few days later Jack was back from his trip and with only a few days left of winter break, we didn't waste any time talking about what was new. We fell right back into our video games and other winter break activities.

It was when we got back to school that I remember I still

had not called Piper. I had hoped I would see her in one of my classes or in the hall so I could talk to her again and apologize for not calling. Unfortunately, that was not the case. I had been to all my morning classes, no Piper. When the lunch bell rang, I had renewed hope that I would see her wandering around the lunchroom, looking for a friendly face and a place to sit.

I rushed through the lunch line and started walking to the table Jack and I always sat at when I saw them. Piper and Jack sitting closely together laughing and my heart sank. I slowly walked over to the table, when Jack looked up and saw me, his smile said it all.

Hour Two

My thoughts are interrupted when Abby goes to the cafeteria to get us some food. We nibble here and there, but none of us seems to have an appetite. It does not take long for my memories to float back to the past.

After that lunch Piper and Jack were inseparable. I soon became the third wheel. My thoughts would wander back and forth to what could have been. If I would have just told Jack about Piper when he got back from vacation, he would have known I liked her. After Jack found out Piper and I had already met at the movies, he asked me if I was interested. He offered to back off if I was. I told him no, I wasn't interested. It was not a hard lie to convince him of since I hadn't called her and I hadn't told him about her. He, like a good friend, asked if I was sure before he asked her out. I stupidly assured him I was.

When Jack told me Piper was pregnant and that he would not be going to college, I decided to stay here with them. Some would call me a masochist for wanting to stay, but I could not leave my best friend behind while I went off and followed our "dreams." College was not for me anyways, I was only going because all three of us were. My life was here, it always had been.

Hour Three

Bryna finally falls asleep in Casey's arms. Casey had been comforting her when the need for sleep overcame her will to stay awake. I watch as Casey gently caresses Bryna's hair. It reminds me of Piper and Jack the day Bryna was born.

Piper had a very long, hard labor with Bryna. Jack and I had been taking turns listening to Piper yell at us as we waited for her to fully dilate. Piper did not have and still does not have a tolerance for pain. Jack had just sent me to get us some coffee. The hospital coffee was horrible so I would drive over to a cafe a few blocks away to get the good stuff. When I got back, the door was closed and a nurse let me know Piper was in full labor and it could be a while. I took a seat in the waiting room and waited. Part of me was happy for them. They were about to become a family. The other part of me was still jealous. Not because I wanted to be a young father, but because I wanted it to be me and Piper, not Jack and Piper. I had been in love with Piper since the day I met her.

Jack came out to tell me that they had a healthy baby girl. I jumped from my seat and gave him a huge hug, congratulating him. He invited me back into the room to meet Bryna. I told him I needed to use the bathroom and would be right in. His excitement was contagious, but I still needed a minute to prepare.

When I walked into the room Jack was seated on the bed next to Piper. He was resting his head on hers and he was stroking her hair. They were both looking at a now-sleeping Bryna. I stood in the doorway for a few moments watching them. They were in love, and not the starry-eyed puppy love kind. You could tell that they were really in love. I knew right then that no matter my feelings, they were meant to be together and I would do everything I could to help them stay that happy.

Hour Four

Part of me hoped that the doctor would be coming out at any moment to tell us that everything went perfectly and that the surgery was already over. When the doctor did not come out with news, I could not stop my mind from remembering the day Jack found out my true feelings.

After my dad died, he left me a larger inheritance. I could have done many things with the money but I went to Jack with a plan to open our own business. When I told him my plan was to make him a 50 percent partner, he couldn't understand why. After an hour of listening to my halfhearted reasons, he started to get pissed. He thought I was giving him a handout. Jack was a proud man and was never one to accept handouts of any kind.

Despite my attempts to convince him that it was not a handout and that his experience was worth a 50 percent partnership, he almost stormed out. I had no choice but to tell him the truth. I told him about the day I met Piper and how I instantly fell in love with her and that I let my stupidity get in the way of what could have been.

Jack was speechless. He had no idea how I had felt about Piper for all these years. He allowed me to tell him that it was never my intention to tell him how I felt about her and that my friendship with the both of them meant more to me than anything in the world. I confided in him that part of the reason I wanted to start the business with him was so that he and Piper wouldn't have to worry about money should the business take off and do well. I wanted them to be happy.

Jack agreed to go into business with me and to never tell Piper about my feelings. I wanted everything to remain the same. I did not want anything to be weird with us so Jack agreed to never speak of it again.

Hour Five

More food. After Bryna woke, she made a small comment that her stomach was empty and Abby took that as a cue to bring more food. This time, it looks like she brought back the whole cafeteria. The smell finally gets to all of us and we are able to fill our bellies.

Hour Six

The feeling that something is going wrong is overwhelming. I don't let my fear be seen by Bryna or anyone but it is there pulling at my insides. There should have been an update of some kind by now. A few words to let us know the surgery is going as planned with no complications. The feelings brought me back to the day Jack died.

I was in the office when I heard the crash. I looked outside and saw that it was Jack's car. I don't remember running outside to the car, but before I knew it, I was at his side. Blood was everywhere. I tried to open the smashed car door, but it would not budge. I ran around to the passenger side and crawled in to see if I could help him. I heard a man yell to me that an ambulance was on the way.

I remember telling Jack to hold on, that help was coming. However, I could see it in his eyes. He knew he would not make it. I was not willing to believe my best friend was going to die in front of me. I ordered him to fight, to stay alive as he was gasping for air. The minutes felt like hours. I could hear the sirens in the distance getting closer but I could see my friend slipping further and further way. His breathing was starting to slow, his eyes were starting to dim. He reached for my hand.

"Take care of them," he whispered.

"Don't talk like that, you are going to be just fine, just hold on."

"Flynn, I'm not."

"Yes you are. You can't leave yet."

"We had a good run."

"And it's not over yet, there is still more to do," I tell him.

"You will have to do it without me," he says, coughing.

"Jack, don't you dare leave."

"Flynn, it's my time. Promise me you will take care of them."

"Jack I'm not you, they need you."

"I will always be with them, but now I need you to be the man in their life. I wouldn't trust anyone else."

"Jack, no."

"Promise me," he whispers even quieter.

"I promise, I will watch out for them," I tell him as the tears start to fall from my eyes.

He smiled one last smile before closing his eyes and fading away.

I cannot help but think that I have failed Jack in some way. I promised I would take care of Piper and Bryna and here we are waiting as Piper fights for her life.

.

Hour Seven

This is going to kill me. I need to know everything is going okay. How can they leave us sitting here for seven fucking hours with no word whatsoever? The only thing keeping me from exploding is the old saying, no news is good news.

I'm pacing the room for the ten-thousandth time when Doctor Redding finally comes into the waiting room. Everyone is on their feet eager to hear how it all went.

"She did great," she tells us.

"Thank God," we all seem to call out in unison.

"There were no complications to Piper or to Helen. They should both recover nicely," she continues.

"When can we see her?" I ask.

"They are moving her to the ICU so we can monitor her. You will also be happy to know that we are discontinuing the propofol for the induced coma. If all else goes well, she should be awake in a few hours. We will keep you posted and let know you know when you can see her.

"Flynn, now that you know she is going to be fine you need to get some sleep," Casey tells me.

"I'm fine. I want to wait until I can talk to her," I inform her.

"Okay, I was trying not to say anything, but you look like shit. You need to go home, take a shower, and get some sleep. You heard the doctor, you have a few hours. Go. We will call you when she wakes up," she insists.

I know she is right. I have been here in the same clothes since yesterday afternoon. The last thing I want is for Piper to wake up to some scruffy bum who smells like hospital food.

Rae Matthews

Chapter Twenty-Nine

Carpe Diem

~ *Piper* ~

I can feel the ache of my body as I start to wake. I don't remember going to bed. The last thing I remember was the large tree branch trying to kill me. My eyelids are heavy and do not want to open. My mind is foggy. It's hard to concentrate. My mind is drifting in and out until I hear my name.

"Piper, can you hear me?" a voice calls.

There is now a bright light flashing in my eyes.

"Hi there, welcome back to us," a woman dressed in scrubs tells me as she put what looks like a small flashlight in her pocket.

"What? Where? Who?"

"Take your time, don't rush it. I am Doctor Redding here at Heartland Community Hospital. You have been through quite an ordeal."

"What happened?" I ask softly.

"You were in a car accident," she tells me.

"Am I dead?" I ask, still confused.

"No, you are not dead. You have been asleep for a little

while, though."

"Dinner, I need you to call…" I rattle in a foggy panic.

"It's okay, Piper, your family is here. We will explain everything to you in time, right now I want you to get some more rest," she tells me.

"All right, but someone needs to cancel the reservations," I mumble before closing my eyes.

"Mom, can you hear me?" I hear Bryna call.

I open my eyes slowly. When I am able to focus, I see her beautiful smiling face.

"Hi, honey. I'm sorry we didn't get dinner. I can make a frozen pizza when we get home," I tell her.

She lets out a small laugh through what looks like tears.

"Honey, why are you crying? I'm fine. See," I say as I try to sit up.

A searing pain like I have never felt before courses through my abdomen, urging me to stay still.

"Maybe I will *just* lie here a while longer," I tell her as I lie back.

"Mom, take it easy, you had major surgery."

Surgery? What? Looking around the room, I see the tearful eyes of everyone, everyone but Flynn. What the hell happened to me? Why did I need surgery?

"What are you talking about?"

"Mom, you've been in a medically induced coma for a month and today you had a liver transplant," Bryna tells me.

"What? No, I was just, I was just." The shock takes over when I realize I can't remember.

"Mom, it's alright. You're going to be fine."

"What happened?"

"The police said you were parked on the side of the road, the other car lost control when it started to hydroplane," Abby tells me.

"What about the other person, are they okay?"

"Yes, they are fine. But your liver was damaged and you needed a transplant," she tells me.

My eyes start to fill with tears. The thought that I could have left my little girl here alone breaks my heart, and on the anniversary of her father's death.

"Honey, I am so sorry," I tell her.

"Mom, you're going to be fine."

"Bryna, I'm sorry, I shouldn't have…" I start.

"Mom, there is more. There was a mass on your liver. They are sending it out for testing," she tells me.

"Cancer?" I ask.

"They haven't said one way or the other, just that more tests were needed."

"The thought of you being here to deal with this, all by yourself," I say as I start to cry.

"I wasn't. Abby and Casey have been great, and Flynn has been by my side and yours the whole time.

I look around the room again, where is Flynn, did I not see him? I look and look, no Flynn.

"Where is he?" I ask.

"I sent him home to shower. He looked and smelled like a hobo." Abby laughs.

"He is on his way back now," Bryna tells me, smiling.

Doctor Redding comes back to check on me and asks everyone to leave to allow me to rest some more. I kiss everyone good-bye. Each of them tells me they will check back in a few hours after they get some sleep.

My eyes close and my thoughts are running wild. A month. I've been asleep for a month. I have a new liver. Holy crap this is a lot to take in. I feel a tear start to escape my eye and then a warm hand wipes it away.

I open my eyes to see Flynn sitting next to me. His face doesn't hide his exhaustion. It almost looks as if he has aged five years overnight.

"Hi," he says softly.

"Hi." I smile.

"You gave us quite a scare," he tells me.

"Well, it was the only way I could get you to talk to me," I joke.

"Piper, there are better ways to do that." He laughs softly.

"Flynn, I am so sorry," I start.

"Piper no, I was the jackass here."

"But I shouldn't have…"

"It doesn't matter, all that matters is that I still have you. Who gives a shit about all that other crap?"

"You had every right to be mad, I should not have read the letter. It was your letter."

"It wasn't you reading the letter that got to me."

"But—"

"I was going to wait until it was the right time, but when is the time right to tell your best friend's widow that I am in love with her."

The words hang in the air, as he waits for my reaction.

"Piper, I was scared that you reading the letter would give my feelings for you away."

"I don't understand."

"I know that I can never and will never replace Jack. He was my best friend, and I know this seems wrong, but I'm in love with you. I have been in love with you for years if I am being honest, and Jack knew that. That is why in his letter he mentioned that I would have his blessing."

It all makes sense now—he was scared I would find out he has loved me all this time.

"I have wanted to tell you for months now, but I could never bring myself to say the words. It felt so wrong. Even with his letter, it was as if I was cheating on my friend, but seeing you here and almost losing you, I can't hold it any longer. I need you to know how much I have loved you," Flynn confesses.

"I… I… I don't know what to say," I say, stuttering.

"Then don't say anything, but I want you to know that if

you do not feel the same way, this will be the first and the last time I tell you. I don't want to ruin our friendship," Flynn continues.

"No, I mean I don't know what to say because I do feel the same way. I didn't know what to do with these feelings, that is why I stopped us that night. I also felt like I was betraying Jack," I offer as my own confession.

Flynn does not say a word. A single tear runs down his cheek. I reach over to wipe it away and with that, he brings his lips to mine. A kiss so pure and so passionate that any pain I was feeling melts away.

As he pulls away, my eyes open. I get a faint scent of coffee. Jack? I feel like he is here and I don't know why, but I get a sense that this is okay. That Jack would be okay with this, is almost a feeling of being at peace. I look into Flynn's eyes and take a deep breath. I know that Jack will never leave my heart. He will always be a part of me.

I think back to that day at the cemetery with Bryna. I told her that if I found someone worthy enough of sharing my heart, I would consider it. Today I realized I found someone who is worthy of sharing it.

Rae Matthews

Chapter Thirty
No Pain, No Gain

Three months have flown by since my release from the hospital. Today marks the one-year anniversary of my Carpe Diem adventure. So much has happened in the last year it is hard to keep track of. In what seems like yesterday, I was given the gift Jack could not by the people in my life that loved Jack as much as I did. They followed me along my adventures and created memories that will last a lifetime. But of all the scary things I did this year the scariest was finding out I could have left my little girl here on earth without me. Instead, I found myself, with a new liver. A new liver from the last person on earth I would have expected.

Someone I once hated with every fiber in my body and with such passion, it could have consumed me until the day I died. However, thanks to Jack, Carpe Diem, and the loved ones in my life, I was able to let that hate go. I was able to find myself and my happiness again.

Because of that, I was able to walk in to face Helen and forgive her, even if she could not forgive herself. She needed a way to forgive herself in order to move on to do the one thing I requested of her. Her giving me the liver allowed her that first step. After Helen healed from the surgery, I got a letter from them wishing me the best and letting me know they decided to move out of state to look for a fresh start. I admit I was relieved to get the letter. The thought of running into either of them scared me. I wasn't sure how I should act should that day ever come. I do wish her and Kyle a long and happy life and hope that they are able to move past the last few years.

We found out a week after my transplant that the spot on my liver was early stage liver cancer. It was classified as stage one, but they caught it early with the transplant. Today I am considered cancer free.

It is hard to think that if Jack had not died, if Helen had not been in a coma, I would not have been on the road that night for the truck to have hit me. I may not have found out about the cancer until it was too late. Was this some cosmic plan? Did Jack die so that I could live? I will ask myself these questions for many years to come even though the answers will never come...

As I sit here looking at my list, thinking about Jack, I cannot help but be thankful for the adventures I have had so far and I am hopeful that I will continue to add and cross off things on my list. The last year has opened me back up in ways I never would have thought possible.

Get a tattoo

~~Work at a haunted house~~

~~Create a secret family recipe~~

~~Fun with Girlfriends~~

Fall asleep under the stars

~~Learn to Ski~~

Try Golfing

Complete 25 acts of kindness

Make a difference in someone's life

Take a picture in the same spot in each season

~~Have a whipped cream fight~~
Eat dinner and go to a movie by myself
~~Learn how to shoot a gun~~
Learn to dance
~~Slow dance in the rain~~
~~Sky dive~~
~~Take a cooking class~~
~~Fall in love~~
Marry my best friend
Go on a no limit-shopping spree
Ride in a helicopter
Have a silly day
Write something in wet cement
Have a full moon party
Go skinny-dipping
~~Do a polar plunge~~
Go somewhere tropical
~~Win a contest~~
~~Volunteer my time~~
Watch the sun go down and the stars come out
Learn to knit
Go camping
~~Have my palm read~~
Create a board game
Go apple picking
Plant a garden
Take a Canoe Trip
~~Take a walk with my mom~~
~~Go fishing with my dad~~
~~Eat a six-course meal~~
Go out on a date
Sing Karaoke at a bar
Do something stupid
~~Forgive~~
Find Happiness again

Today I will be crossing off two items. Flynn and Bryna are on their way over to pick me up for our appointment. It has been almost four months since I have been able to cross anything off and I have to make up for lost time.

My recovery has been smooth sailing. My doctor said I should be able to live normally and that she doesn't see anything wrong with my next choice.

"We're here let's get this show on the road!" I hear Bryna announce as she comes through the front door.

"I just have to grab one thing," I call back to her.

I walk to the hutch and grab the plastic bag. There is only one more piece of red mug remaining and it seems fitting that this is the final adventure where I will be leaving a piece of Jack.

"Okay, I'm ready."

Bryna and I walk out to the car where Flynn is waiting for us. I get into the front seat, lean over, and give Flynn a small kiss on the cheek.

"Gross, go get a room will you," Bryna jokes.

"Hey, watch it young lady," I joke back.

Bryna actually couldn't be happier to see Flynn and me together. She likes to joke that it was either him or Channing Tatum and since Channing Tatum is already married and unlikely that I would be able to land him because I am *too old* for him, that Flynn will just have to do.

Whenever the opportunity arrives, she enjoys teasing us about when the wedding date will be. We always laugh and remind her that even though we have known each other a long time, we are not looking to jump into wedding attire just yet. We plan to take it slow. We want to get to know each other in that way. There is no need to rush into anything crazy.

When we pull into the parking lot, we all get a little excited and nervous all at the same time. After all, this *is* a permanent mark on our body. On the count of three, we all jump from the car and make our way to the entrance.

We walk into the small shop filled with wall random art, idea books, and what looks to be piercing jewelry. Rachel, the receptionist, greets us and tells us that Tina will be with is in a moment.

Tina is a kick ass tattoo artist I have been talking to about what kind of tattoo we want. Something simple, but meaningful. She was able to come up with something perfect for me… An outlined coffee cup and the words Carpe Diem curves around as if it was steam.

Bryna designed her own…

Flynn opted to for a very simplistic design…

I had to smirk when I found out why. Flynn is scared to death of needles. I am not sure if I was more shocked that I learned something new or that Flynn is a big huge baby when it comes to tiny pieces of metal with a sharp edge.

As we wait for Tina, I wander around looking at the pick and stick tattoo books. Why someone would willingly choose some of the options is beyond me. The unicorn with a cloud of "fart" coming from its butt or the scary clown face eating a banana. Who in the hell comes up with these ideas.

Flynn is over looking at the piercing jewelry. I put the book down and walk over to him. I take hold of his hand in mine.

"So are you going to man up and get a piercing too?" I joke.

"The test of a real man is not that of the tolerance for pain, the true test is how fast he can run from a man with a needle," he replies.

I laugh loudly, causing Rachel to jump slightly. When I glance her way, she gives a small smile and returns to what she was doing.

"Okay who is ready to get some ink?" Tina calls out as she approaches us.

"I am," I reply.

"Hell yeah," Bryna adds.

"All right who gets to go first?"

Bryna and I both look toward Flynn. We know that after he watches us, he may very well change his mind.

"Oh no, ladies first," he tells us, backing away.

"Flynn, you know you are going to chicken out if you go last," I mock.

He stares at us for a moment, trying to decide if he wants to agree with my point or not I assume. I watch as his eyes soften, victory is mine.

After cleaning Flynn's arm and adding the stencil, Tina makes sure he is ready one last time before she puts the needle to his skin. Flynn nods to her then turns his head. What a baby, I think to myself.

"Ah," he calls out as Tina turns on the machine.

"Dude, I haven't even touched you yet," Tina tells him.

"I know, I was just practicing," he jokes.

Ten short minutes later, Flynn is done. He was a champion—no yelling, no screaming, and no twitching. Tina even gave him a Dum Dum sucker. It was meant as a joke, but he paraded it around like it was the Stanley Cup.

I went next. I could not handle the anticipation any longer, it was killing me. Tina follows her routine of prepping the area, my right ankle, and starts the machine once again. It was a strange sensation. It didn't feel as if my skin was being punctured over and over by a small needle pushing ink into my skin, it felt, to me, like steady vibration.

It does not take Tina long to finish my tattoo, maybe a half hour. When I stand and look in the mirror, I smile at its perfection. Bryna starts clapping and I watch as her eyes fill with tears. Mine don't take long to follow. A quick hug and it is Bryna's turn. Flynn and I stand back and compare notes on the experience.

"I'm happy to see you could handle the pain," he tells me.

"Excuse me?" I ask.

"You know being a girl and all, I was thinking I would see you faint or something," he jokes.

"Well, let's see you give birth to a watermelon after they shove a giant needle in your back, then you can talk to me about pain," I joke back.

"Fine, you win." He chuckles and then pulls me closer to gives me a kiss.

Bryna's tattoo took a little longer because of the two shades, but looking at the beauty resting on her forearm, it was well worth it.

Before leaving, I offer Tina the remaining piece of Jack's glass. Tina already knew most of my story but didn't know about the mug until now. When I finish telling her and place it in her hand, there is not a dry eye in the house.

Carpe Diem may have started out a silly school assignment a substitute teacher gave me, but today I plan to Carpe the hell out of each Diem until my last breath.

Once my tattoo is complete, I pull out my folded list and find what I am looking for at the top of my list and cross it off.

Get a tattoo

Next, I look to the end of the list and find the next thing I intend to cross off today.

Find Happiness again

Epilogue
One Year Later

What a year it has been. Bryna graduated from college with honors, moved back home, and Flynn has her helping at Avery Reynolds Excavating & Landscape Services. She has amazing ideas about how to expand the business and Flynn tells me if she keeps up the enthusiasm he may retire and let her take over.

I can't say I hate that idea. Flynn and I have been busy adding and crossing things off the Carpe Diem list, but work does tend to put a damper on plans from time to time. However, not today. Today I cross the final item off from my original list. Flynn and I had managed to do everything else over the last year and today seems the perfect day to finish.

Three months ago on a short trip to Jamaica, Flynn proposed. We were stuck in our hotel room because of rain. We didn't mind. We spent the evening talking and laughing for hours. We eventually ordered room service, adding a side of strawberries and champagne. A little cliché I know, but I loved everything about it.

When the conversation seemed to fade, I was surprised when Flynn put on some soft music then took my hand in his and brought me out on to the balcony. He looked into my eyes and danced in the rain.

"Piper, I have loved you since the first day I saw you. You are the most beautiful woman I have ever known. Being with you makes me the happiest man in the world. Do you know how much I love you?"

"Yes I do, and I love you," I reply.

"I want to spend the rest of my life dancing with you. I want to seize each day, together... wherever the adventure brings us I want to be at your side... Marry me."

"Yes. Yes," I shouted.

He placed a ring on my finger, we made love under the stars, and today we will say, "I do."

Neither of us wanted a large wedding. We decided something small with our closest friends and family was more us. Chef Basil was more than ecstatic when I called and asked him to cater the wedding for us. Unfortunately, Flynn made him promise no Spam. I was a little disappointed, so Chef made sure to sneak in a Spam-inspired hors d'oeuvre for me.

"Mom, it's almost time," Bryna announces as she comes into the bedroom.

"Thank you, sweetie."

"Mom, you look amazing," she says, smiling.

"You don't look bad yourself." I smile.

"Are you ready?" she asks.

"Ready as I will ever be," I say as a few tears start to form.

"No, you're not allowed to cry yet, you will ruin your makeup," she says and the tears form in her eyes.

We each begin to laugh and wipe away our tears.

"We better you get down there before this turns into a full on cry fest," Abby calls from the doorway.

"What is a wedding without a few tears of joy," I tell her.

"Well, you can cry all the tears of joy you want after the pictures. It took me an hour to do your makeup and it is a work of art that cannot be duplicated," she jokes.

The three of us begin down the stairs and meet Casey in the living room where she is waiting to hand me my bouquet. She is not having an easy time holding back her tears when she sees me making my way down the staircase.

"Breathtaking," she calls out.

"Ah, you're just saying that," I joke.

"Bryna, isn't your mom breathtaking?"

After a few hugs, a few more tears, and a quick wardrobe check, we are making our way to the back door. The backyard has been transformed into the perfect stage for our I do's. It was nearly dusk, the white lights that hang are starting to glow with the setting sun. The band starts to play when Casey signals them we are ready. I catch a glimpse of Flynn standing next to the officiate, waiting for me to walk down the aisle.

He looks so handsome in his tuxedo, and I can't wait to be standing next to him. As Bryna and I start to walk toward him, I resist the urge to run down the aisle, partly because I know it is not a race to the finish line and partly because I know Bryna has been looking forward to walking me down the aisle to give me away.

"Who gives this woman to be wed?" the officiate asks.

"I do," Bryna replies.

Bryna places my hand in Flynn's and then takes her seat.

Flynn and I stare into each other's eyes and everyone and everything fades away. It is as if it is just the two of us here. If it were not for the vows we are to repeat, I would not have heard a word that was said.

"I, Piper, take you Flynn to be my husband, to be my faithful partner in life. I will stand by your side and sleep in your arms through sickness and in health, in joy and in sorrow. I promise to love you without reservation, to live with you and laugh with you through the best and worst. I will always be open and honest with you, and cherish you for as long as we both shall live."

"I, Flynn, take you Piper to be my wife, to be my faithful partner in life. I will stand by your side and sleep in your arms through sickness and in health, in joy and in sorrow. I promise to love you without reservation, to live with you and laugh with you through the best and worst. I will always be open and honest with you, and cherish you for as long as we both shall live."

"With that, I present to you Mr. and Mrs. Avery. Sir, you may now kiss your bride."

Flynn takes me into his arms, places his hand on my cheek, and kisses me with such tenderness. It isn't until Abby gave an "ahem" that we realize the kiss lasted a little longer than it should have.

Flynn and I walk back down the aisle while everyone claps. I can feel my cheeks warm with embarrassment, but I don't care. I am in love, and I am happy.

The evening flies by in a blur. Chef Basil outdid himself with our meal, the band played well past the time they were to end, and no one could say they didn't have a wonderful time. When the last guest finally leaves, Flynn and I fall down on the soft grass.

"You're stuck with me now," he tells me.

"Ha, jokes on you, tomorrow I'm putting yoga pants on and I'm never taking them off."

"You look good in yoga pants," he tells me.

"Yeah, right. Only supermodels and yoga instructors look good in yoga pants."

"You can be my yoga instructor," he jokes.

"Ha, right, you can't even do downward facing whatever."

Flynn smiles as he pulls a folded piece of paper from his pocket.

"Well, before you teach me downward facing whatever, would you like to do the honors?"

I carefully unfold the delicate paper and find the last item that needs to be crossed off.

~~Marry my best friend~~

The End...

Rae Matthews

Bonus Chapter
Dream A Little Dream

The smell of coffee fills the room. My eyes are closed, and I keep them closed a few moments longer, taking deep breaths and enjoying the aroma. Tossing the comforter off me, I jump from my bed, I quickly change into jeans and a tee shirt before heading downstairs.

As I come around the corner, I see Jack sitting at the dining room table reading a book and sipping coffee from his favorite red mug. He hasn't heard or seen me yet so I tiptoe softly and sneak up behind him.

"I wouldn't do that if I were you," he tells me.

"Oh come on, how did you know I was there?"

"Because I was a ninja in a former life," he jokes.

"Ninja my ass."

"If I told you my secrets, I would have to kill you," he jokes again.

"So what are we going to do today?" I ask.

"Oh, I thought we would take a walk and then have a picnic."

"Really? It's a little cold out for a picnic don't you

think?" I ask.

"No, it's a beautiful day," he informs me.

I walk to the front door and walk out onto the porch. The sky is blue, the trees are full of leaves, and there is a soft breeze kissing my cheek. I have a strange feeling that something is not right. I could have sworn it was going to be cool today.

Jack wraps his arms around me and kisses my neck.

"See, told you."

"I will make the sandwiches you grab the blanket and wine."

"No need, everything is ready."

"Did you plan this?" I question with squinty eyes.

"Just go with it."

Jack grabs a basket from the kitchen and we begin walking down to the park. We don't say much, just walking hand in hand with him is enough. The streets are quiet. Not another person is seen, odd but seems meant to be. I can't remember the last time Jack and I took a picnic to the park.

Normally I would have expected to see children playing at the playground on a day like today so it is strange when, again, I do not see anyone when we arrive at the park. I brush it off and help Jack lay out the blanket.

"So what brought this on?" I ask.

"I just thought you would enjoy spending the day together."

I feel as if he has something up his sleeve. Jack is a sweet man but romance has never been his strong suit.

"Jack, what did you do?" I joke.

"I didn't *do* anything, why would you think that?" He laughs.

"Oh I don't know, you tell me?"

"What, a guy can't do something nice for his wife once in a while?"

"No, not really?" I tease.

Jack smiles because he knows I am right, but not another

word is said about it. We sit down to snack on the fruit and bread he packed. We laugh and talk for what seems like hours but the sun never seems to move. Jack and I have never had a hard time when together. Some couples complain about how when you get older and have been married for twenty years that it seems you run out things to talk about. Not Jack and me. Maybe it is because we were so young when we met. We have been through everything together, and we share everything with each other.

It isn't until I realize I haven't seen anyone since we have been here that I feel something is not right.

"Jack?"

"Yes?"

"Do you realize that we have been here for hours and haven't seen a soul?" I ask.

"Yes."

"How is that possible?"

There is a long pause.

"Jack? What is going on?"

"Everything is fine, you are going to be fine."

"Jack, please tell me what is going on."

It is then that the past comes flooding back to me. Jack died, I am a widow…wait, the car lights are coming at me.

"Wait, you're… am I…?"

"No, Piper, you are going to be just fine."

"But I…"

My heart starts to race, my palms start to sweat, and my skin feels like it is crawling.

"Piper, it's okay, calm down. You are going to be just fine."

"But how, how are you here, how am I here, is this a dream?" I ask, panicking.

"Piper, you don't belong here. You are going to leave here soon and be just fine."

Wait, what, leave Jack, again? I can't lose him again.

"No I want to stay, I want to stay with you."

"Piper, Bryna needs you. Flynn needs you. You have to go back."

"But I need you, Jack," I say as the tears fall from my cheeks.

"Piper, I love you, I will always love you. But it's almost time for you to go home."

"I am home, I am with you."

I suddenly feel very light, like my body could at any moment float away. Jack pulls me into his arms and holds me tight. His embrace feels so warm, I do not ever want him to let go. He looks at me one last time and brings his lips to mine. As the light takes over, I can hear Jack's final words to me as if they are floating on the wind.

"Seize the day, Piper. Be happy. Know that I will always love you. I will be at your side giving you my blessing to be happy once again."

I can feel the ache of my body as I start to wake. I don't remember going to bed. The last thing I remember was the large tree branch trying to kill me. My eyelids are heavy and do not want to open. My mind is foggy. It's hard to concentrate. My mind is drifting in and out until I hear my name.

"Piper, can you hear me?" a voice calls.